He's a She!

In an instant, Michelle's adrenaline kicked into overdrive. With no time to think, she zoomed toward the Atom player until—*whomp!* She hit a brick wall and was out like a light.

When she came to, faces swarmed above her. Voices echoed. And that was only the beginning of her worst nightmare.

She'd lost her helmet.

The whole world, including Coach Brown, was peering down at a girl grotesquely disguised as a guy with masking-taped hair. Michelle closed her eyes tight. Maybe when she woke up, this would all be a dream. Sadly, it wasn't.

"Cripes! Look at that!" Joey's obnoxious voice rang out above the crowd. "Hey, you guys. Helmet Head's a Conehead. And he's a she! And she's a girl!"

Get That GIRL Out of the BOYS' LOCKER ROOM!

ELAINE MOORE

Troll

If you want to find out more about Elaine Moore, look on the World Wide Web at www.elainemoore.com

For Bill Renner, football coach,
Langley High School, Fairfax County, Virginia

CHAPTER 1

"**F**or a truly beautiful body, grab each wrist with the opposite hand and lock your hands tight," Sandy said with a perky toss of her ponytail. "Pay attention, Michelle. If we don't do this right, we have no idea how our bodies might turn out. Let's do it together. Are you with me? Now grab. One . . . two . . . oooh!"

Michelle, sitting cross-legged on a red-and-white picnic blanket with Sandy and her other best friend, Skye, knew she was running out of time. All summer long, she'd measured herself on her bedroom wall. Talk about the agony of defeat. In two months, two weeks, and five days, she hadn't grown a millimeter beyond four feet nine inches. It was a sure bet Michelle Dupree would be the tiniest seventh grader at Jefferson Junior High. Most likely she'd be even dinkier than the newbie sixth graders.

Michelle's face paled at the thought. What if someone mistook her for a leftover from fourth grade? Michelle shook her head, shuddered, and locked her hands tightly around her wrists. According to Sandy, her only salvation rested in the seven-day miracle exercise program they had discovered only an hour before at the supermarket.

"What a deal," Sandy had gushed when they spotted the palm-sized paperback in the wire rack above the checkout counter. "Here, I'll treat. How can I resist? This is probably the best investment we'll ever make. Three beautiful bodies for only a dollar ninety-nine."

"Michelle!" Sandy's reprimand jolted Michelle out of her daydream. "You're at least six grabs behind. Come on, this is really important! We must . . . We must . . . We must improve our bust," she chanted.

In the distance, Michelle's older brother, Brian, was playing football with some seventh- and eighth-grade boys, including Michelle's friend Matt. For the moment, neither she, nor Sandy, nor Skye was paying much attention as they sat on their blanket and exercised in the park. They were too busy concentrating on their own soon-to-be-truly-beautiful bodies.

Sandy stopped chanting about busts. "Step two. 'Make sure your forearms are level with your shoulders,'" she read. "'Push and hold for a count of five.'"

"Wait a second." Skye sounded frantic. "I can't see the picture. Turn the book around. I might be doing it wrong." She anchored the book with one of her long legs.

All three girls pushed while Sandy counted. "One and two and three and—"

"Brian does this all the time," Michelle interrupted. "I've seen him in front of his mirror."

"For his breasts?" Sandy asked, losing count.

Giggling, Michelle released her grip and rolled backward on the blanket. "No, silly. For his pecs. Guys are really hot on building their pectoral muscles."

"Oooh, I think I feel something." Sandy's eyes opened wide.

"Me, too," Skye said. "How many times are you supposed to do this? I don't want to injure myself."

Michelle crossed her eyes and pulled her T-shirt away from her body in two empty points. "Va-voom. Va-voom. Morning, noon, and night," she answered before turning back to Sandy. "This year the whole world is going to know me as a seventh-grade *girl*."

Sandy grabbed Michelle's hands. "There's no way anyone's going to mistake you for a boy. Not with those fingernails. Just look at them. They're even longer than mine."

Sandy was right. Never a fingernail freak before, for the past two months, two weeks, and five days Michelle had cultivated her nails like a summer garden. She'd used almond cuticle conditioner. She'd polished her nails with Mauve Allure and shaped them. Of course, it was only temporary. She'd have to file them down when she went out for basketball—a willing sacrifice.

"I'm still chewing mine," Skye said, interrupting Michelle's thoughts. "It's okay. I read somewhere that they're no-fat. Do you think guys notice? They're always so busy showing off. Just look at them now playing football. They keep turning to see if we're watching."

"Yeah," Sandy said, smiling. "Check it out."

No one breathed a word. Finally, Sandy mused to no one in particular, "I wonder if we'll win any games this year. All our good players, like Brian and Derek, are on the high-school team now."

"So?" Michelle said. "We still have plenty of good players."

"Name one," Sandy demanded.

"Matt's out there."

"And Lamar and Rani," Skye added.

Sandy shook her head. "I don't think so. Lamar and Rani are okay, but Matt didn't play football for the Eagles last year. Just because you and he were on the basketball team together doesn't mean he'll be good in football. He's not exactly big and burly."

"Right," Michelle jumped in. "But he's smart and fast on his feet. Brian says it's a sure thing he'll be quarterback. Maybe even team captain."

"Oooh," Sandy said, impressed.

"Speaking of basketball," Skye interrupted, "are you going out for the team again this year, Michelle? If you do, I will, but I don't want to try out by myself."

Sandy pulled Jefferson's back-to-school information packet from her purse. "Did you check to see if there is even going to be a basketball team?"

For a minute, the color drained from Skye's face. Clearly, playing on Jefferson's basketball team last year had meant the world to her.

"Don't worry." Michelle read the printed pages over Sandy's shoulder. "It says here that because of continued budget considerations, there will be only one co-ed basketball team. Same as last year," she added.

Sandy folded the sheets of paper. "I guess that means you two are headed for the boys' locker room again. You guys have all the luck."

"Me and Smidge, right, Michelle?"

"Stop it! This year I don't want to be called Smidge. It's cute but it sounds like a boy's name. Now that I'm in seventh grade, I'd rather be called Michelle."

"I wouldn't care what they called me if they let me in the boys' locker room. It's not fair." Sandy stood up, put her hands behind her head, and stretched. "It's not fair that only jocks—excuse me, Michelle—are allowed in the boys' locker room."

"Honestly, Sandy, it's no big deal. You've seen one toilet, you've seen them all."

Skye's mouth dropped. "I don't think we should be talking about"—she looked around and whispered—"boys' toilets."

"Well, it would be a big deal if you'd never been there," Sandy said, ignoring Skye. "But that's okay. Because this year I'm going to be a sports reporter. That will get me in the boys' locker room, guaranteed. And furthermore," Sandy added, pausing for emphasis, "I intend to be a good sports reporter." She tightened her ponytail. "I saw those football diagrams on TV. All those cute little X's and O's. You know, like kisses and hugs."

Michelle couldn't believe her ears. "Kisses and hugs? X's and O's are part of a coach's game plan," Michelle shouted. "It's his chalkboard talk, not a love note!"

Just then a football plopped on the ground near them.

"Smidge! Smi-i-i-i-dge!" Downfield, big mouth Brian was shouting and waving his arms. "Hey, Smidge. Send it over here."

Michelle stood up and dusted off her shorts. It was too far to walk. Besides that, it was too hot. Why couldn't lazybones Brian come and get the ball himself?

Grumbling under her breath, Michelle picked up the ball.

"Over here, Smidge!" Brian yelled louder. Matt and Derek were waving their arms, too.

11

Michelle twirled the ball in the soft earth until it was propped up at a slight angle. She backed up, took a couple steps, and gave it a sound kick. Then she turned around and headed back for the blanket.

Behind her, she heard a loud cheer.

Sandy's hand was over her mouth. Skye was staring, wide-eyed and dumbstruck.

"Do you know what you just did?" Sandy said finally.

"Yeah, I kicked the ball to bigmouth Brian. I hope it landed in his water-bucket mouth."

"It didn't," Skye said hoarsely. "You just kicked the ball—without even looking, without even trying, without even aiming—right between the uprights."

CHAPTER 2

"**W**ow, Michelle! You are just what we need!" Matt was grinning from ear to ear. His face was red, but it couldn't have been from playing hard. He wasn't out of breath, even though he had sprinted along with the rest of the players to where Michelle, Sandy, and Skye were sitting.

Meanwhile, Derek casually tossed the football from one hand to the other. "I think what Matt means is that Jefferson doesn't have a prayer this year without a decent kicker. So far the only man they've got is Joey."

"Yeah, Jocko Joey. He can't kick a tin can across the street without stubbing his toe," Lamar said.

"Cool it," Matt interrupted. "We all know he'd make better plays on defense, but getting him to accept that is impossible."

"Well, you better think of a way," Rani grumbled. "Because it looks like Coach is going to make you quarterback. Maybe even captain."

"Really?" Michelle said, her face heating up too. "That's great."

"What's Jocko Joey got to do with Michelle?" Sandy wanted to know.

"Yeah," Michelle said. "Why are you guys giving me strange looks all of a sudden?"

"Because, twerp," Brian said loudly, "you just walloped the ball from at least forty-five yards."

"Yeah, and your aim wasn't all that bad either," Matt added.

"Big deal." Michelle rolled her eyes. "I do it all the time."

"You what?" Matt blinked. Michelle couldn't tell if he was impressed or surprised. "You do?"

"Sure. Ask Brian."

Puzzled, Lamar shoved Brian's shoulder. "You holding out on us, man?"

Brian stopped wiping the sweat off his face with the bottom of his T-shirt and flung his arms in the air, feigning innocence. "Hey, when you asked if I knew any good kickers, you never said *girls*. She used to kick the ball around when we were kids and Dad was helping me learn how to block and tackle. How was I supposed to know she kept it up? I'm only her brother. Give me a break."

It was like a tennis match. Now everyone was staring at Michelle again.

"Well, I didn't exactly keep it up," she said honestly. "I mean, I didn't kick all that much. Only sometimes. Like when I was mad at Brian about something. You know, like if he stuffed one of his grungy socks in my lunch bag."

Brian made a goofier face than usual. "Okay, so maybe that's five times a week for starters, and that's only if I change my socks."

A couple of guys laughed, but not Matt. He got right down to business. "So, will you do it?" he asked Michelle, his brown eyes begging like a cocker spaniel's.

When Michelle looked at him, she couldn't help but smile. The tops of his ears were still pink, his light brown hair fell over his forehead, and there was a faint sprinkling of freckles dancing across his nose. He was so cute, he made her heart pound. But what was he talking about? "Do what?" she asked.

"Try out for the team, man," Lamar shouted, bringing her out of her Matt-induced trance.

"You're forgetting about Coach Brown," Rani lamented. "Unlike your basketball coach, he's not very cool when it comes to girl athletes."

"Oh, yeah, Michelle," Matt groaned. "Major obstacle. This morning he called Rani a powder puff when he dropped the ball."

"I couldn't help it," Rani explained. "I got ambushed by a steamroller."

"Coach told me I'd have a hard time making the Lipstick League when I couldn't get a first down with three tacklers hanging on each ankle." Lamar shook his head in disgust. "Man, it'll be a hot day in January before Coach Brown lets girls on his team. I don't care how good they are."

"Too bad for him," Sandy said with a shake of her shoulders. "Sounds like a personal problem to me."

Michelle shifted her weight to one leg and folded her arms across her chest. Why should she even care? Putting on bulky shoulder pads, hot Spandex pants, and an oversized jersey just to play football with a bunch of sweaty boys was not exactly her idea of fun.

Derek spun the football in the air and caught it. "Well, too bad you guys are going to get creamed this year. I'm telling you, Matt, you don't stand a chance without a decent kicker."

Michelle could tell by the way he arched his eyebrows that what he'd said was for her benefit.

Brian agreed. "The Barracudas will grind you up like dog meat. And I, for one, am ready to see the Barracudas eat mud after what they did to us last year."

Unable to resist, Michelle piped up. "We got them under the net. What more do you want?"

Derek shook his head. "That was basketball. Everyone knows it's not the same."

Skye pursed her lips as she looked at Derek. If eyes could have shot daggers, Derek would have been a goner. "The same as what?" she demanded.

"Football," Brian shouted back.

Nobody said anything for a few minutes until Rani whispered, "Yeah, football."

Derek took a deep breath and smiled at Skye. "You might not think so, but football is a hundred times tougher than basketball."

"More physical," Lamar explained.

"That's not true," Michelle snapped, defending her favorite sport. "Basketball gets pretty physical. Plus it's faster. Besides, the way you guys play football, you spend half the time in a huddle and the rest of the time piled up in a heap on the field."

"Yes!" Sandy squealed. "Why do you guys have to huddle so much anyway? Huddle, huddle, huddle, and then heap, heap, heap."

"It doesn't do any good to argue," Matt hollered,

stopping the disagreement before it got any worse. "We won't know anything until I ask Coach Brown at tomorrow's practice."

"Excuse me," Skye interrupted. "We never heard Michelle say she wanted to play your great macho game of football."

Matt turned to look at Michelle. "I'll ask the coach anyway, just in case." His eyes brightened. "I'll give you a call after practice to let you know what he says."

The words had barely left Matt's mouth when Sandy's elbow poked Michelle. "You need her number?" she asked Matt. "I've got paper somewhere inside my purse."

Matt blushed. He pawed the grass with his toe. "No. Um . . . I already have it."

Michelle swallowed hard as she watched Matt and the others head back to their game.

"You know he's going to ask you out," Sandy bubbled as soon as the boys were out of earshot.

"Are you completely nuts?" Michelle exclaimed. "We're not teenagers. Besides, even if he did ask me out, I wouldn't be allowed. Honestly, how many times do I have to tell you? Matt and I are athletes. We're part of a team."

"Team, sheam! The two of you are already an item."

Michelle refused to think about Matt. She wouldn't think about him calling. She wouldn't think about playing football either. Instead, the next morning while Brian was at his high-school football practice and their parents were working at their family rental business, Michelle deliberately kept herself busy. She'd been meaning to take care of a certain problem for a long time.

"Hercules, sit." Hercules, the Duprees' massive golden retriever, whined as he sat down. Sitting was clearly not what he wanted to do. He looked adoringly at Michelle with his big brown eyes.

"Good boy." Michelle patted Hercules on his broad head.

Hercules smiled and panted. He wiggled slightly. "Now stay," Michelle said. Hercules sighed.

"Good boy. Good stay." Michelle held one of Brian's smelly socks in front of Hercules' face. "I'm going to hide this wad of stink and I want you to find it. But not until I say so. You got that, Hercules?"

Hercules barked happily. For a moment he forgot himself and stood up, probably because he had to wag his tail. For a golden retriever like Hercules, tail wagging is difficult to do while sitting down.

"Good boy. Good Hercules," Michelle repeated as soon as Hercules sat back down. "Don't peek," she said as she left the room. Before walking down the hall to her parents' room, she stuck her head back in her room just to be certain Hercules was still sitting there like she'd instructed. He was. If only boys could be as easy to get along with, she thought, as she marched down the hall to her parents' room and tossed the sock under the bed.

Dusting her hands, as though that could rid them of the cooties from Brian's sock, Michelle walked back in her room.

Seeing her, Hercules brushed his tail across the floor. He wiggled, his golden fur rippling in the sun. Michelle knelt down beside him.

"Okay, Herc. Find it," she said.

Hercules looked at her, puzzled. He knew the

commands "sit," "lie down," "speak," and "hush." He knew how to ignore something on the ground when told to "leave it" and how to gently take something in his mouth when told to "take it." He knew how to trot beside a leg when told to "heel." He'd just proven he could stay in one place when told. But "find" was something new. He looked at Michelle and whined. He licked her face.

"Yes, I know. It's a new one," Michelle said. "But you can do it, Hercules. I know you can. Find it! Find Brian's sock." Tugging gently on his collar, she led him to her parents' room. She pointed to the bed. "Find it."

Suddenly, Hercules bounded up on the bed. Waving his tail grandly, he barked happily. Once, twice, three times.

"No, silly!" Michelle clapped her hands and Hercules joined her on the floor. "Find it," she said again, lifting the dust ruffle slightly so the sock was exposed.

Like a golden flash, Hercules snatched the sock in his jaws. He shook it like it was a stinky dead fish.

"Good boy!" Michelle shouted. "You *found* it. Good *find*. Very good *find*." She knelt down on the floor and ruffled his fur, acting like he was the greatest, most brilliant dog in the world, which probably he was.

"Come on," she said. "We're going to do this a few more times so you get the hang of it." She started back toward her room. "Do you have any idea why, Hercules?"

When Hercules didn't answer, Michelle explained. "I'm giving you the opportunity of a lifetime. I'm putting dignity into your life. I'm helping you get a job. When you're trained, it'll be your job to fumigate the house. You'll be Hercules, the Great Fumigator."

Hercules barked twice.

"That's right," Michelle went on. "And all you have to do is sniff out Brian's smelly socks. When you think about it, it's really no different than the way other dogs uncover drugs and explosives. Just because we don't have drugs or explosives in this house doesn't mean you won't be doing a magnificent service. Just think of the sinuses you'll save, Hercules. You'll be a hero!"

Hercules had happily located Brian's sock in the bathtub when the phone rang.

"Okay, so it's good news and bad news," Matt said.

"Am I supposed to choose?" Michelle asked, instantly sorry for sounding so sarcastic. But Matt didn't seem to notice. Neither did Hercules, who, tired of "finding," had rested his head on his paws and gone to sleep on the kitchen floor.

"I'll give you the bad news first," Matt said. "Coach Brown definitely does not want any girls on his team. According to him, it's not a girl's place to play football."

"Huh." Michelle felt the hairs on the back of her neck rise slightly. "Did he say where exactly a girl's place was?"

Matt cleared his throat. "I didn't ask."

Smart, Michelle thought to herself. And if Coach Brown had volunteered the information, Matt was wise enough to keep it to himself. "Okay, so what's the good news?"

"The good news is," Matt went on, "that Lamar, Rani, and I are in complete agreement that we need you on the team."

"And that's supposed to make me feel better?"

Matt's voice squeaked. "It doesn't?"

Michelle reached down and ruffled the fur on

Hercules' back. "Not exactly. I mean, if Coach doesn't want me . . ."

"But, Michelle, you've got to try out."

She tried not to think of Matt's waterfall hair or the cinnamon freckles parading across his nose. "How? You just said Coach—"

"He's not the whole team. He's only one person."

"Right. He's the coach. And the last time I checked, the coach was the boss, not the quarterback."

"Yeah, but we need you. Coach Brown just doesn't know it yet. We already figured out what to do. It won't even be hard. We want you to come and try out as a boy."

"What?" Michelle almost choked. "A boy? Me?"

"Don't worry," Matt said, ignoring her uncertainty. "We'll get you the right equipment. It's like Lamar said. Guys dress up like ladies all the time in the movies."

She could hardly believe what she was hearing. "Well, you better tell Lamar to get a life. This isn't the movies."

"Aw, c'mon, Michelle." Matt was pleading. "It's football and the Eagles. We don't have a shot at winning if you're not on the team. You heard the guys. The only kicker we've got is Jocko Joey, and he's pathetic."

"Listen," Michelle said after a long silence. "You guys are going to get into a lot of trouble if Coach Brown finds out what you're up to. Besides, I don't want to play on a team where I'm not wanted."

"Who said you weren't wanted? I already told you Lamar, Rani, and I want you plenty. We don't care if we get into trouble. It's for the team. Besides, you didn't let anything or anybody stop you last year when it came to playing basketball. We admired that. You're a good kicker. You have to play. Besides," Matt pleaded, "I want you to play. Think how neat it'll be if you're on the team."

Michelle didn't have to ponder what Matt said for very long. Coach Brown's attitude about girl athletes wasn't right. It wasn't even fair. According to her parents, girls deserved respect for their efforts, the same as anyone else. Somebody ought to show Coach Brown that girl athletes were as capable as boy athletes. That somebody ought to be her.

Michelle was shooting baskets in the driveway while Hercules gnawed on a bone when Brian rolled up on his bike.

"You remember what Matt said yesterday about my going out for the Eagles football team?" Michelle asked Brian. She bounced the ball twice and let it sail. *Swish.* "Well, he called a little while ago. He said it didn't matter that the coach doesn't want girls on the team. I could go out for the team dressed up like a guy." She snatched the ball under the net on the first bounce.

When she turned around, Brian was pointing his thumb at his puffed-up chest. "Pretty good idea, huh? It was mine."

Michelle blinked. This was all Brian's idea?

"After I helped Dad stack all the folding chairs at the shop, I just sort of dropped by their practice," Brian said. "You should have seen them. It would have torn your heart out to see Matt, Lamar, and Rani sitting around moaning about Jocko Joey. No sweat, I told them. Plop a helmet on her head and Michelle will make a great guy.

There's no reason in the world anyone would ever suspect she wasn't a boy."

The proud way Brian said it, you would have thought he had scored a perfect round on "Jeopardy."

Michelle stared. Plop a helmet on her head and she'd make a great guy? What about the rest of her body? Was it true that nobody would be able to tell?

Tears rose to Michelle's eyes as her face heated up and her throat closed. How could Brian have said such a humiliating thing? Didn't family loyalty count for anything?

"So I told them," Brian continued as he rolled his bike toward the shed, obviously unaware that he'd caused his sister any pain, "Michelle always plays tough—just like a guy."

Apparently, to Brian, looking and acting like a boy was the highest compliment he could pay his dink little sister.

Like a robot, Michelle headed inside the house with Hercules following close behind. This whole football thing was so confusing. The only thing she knew for certain was that she needed a friend. Michelle headed straight to the phone and dialed Sandy's number.

"What is it? What's the matter?" Sandy asked. "You sound mortally depressed. Like a flat tire."

"I'm flat all right." Michelle sniffed. "According to Brian, I'm flatter than a pancake."

"Don't worry. The exercises are going to work. They are for me. Have you checked your tape measure lately?"

"Honestly, Sandy," Michelle wailed. "There isn't time. I should have started when I was in the cradle. Now, according to Brian, the guys think that because I look like a guy and play like a guy, I ought to *be* a guy."

"That's ridiculous!" Sandy huffed. "Forget football. Where does it say that a girl who can kick perfect field goals must play on the school team? Nowhere."

It was exactly what Michelle needed to hear.

"You're right," Michelle said, feeling much better. "Nobody said I had to do it. So what if the Eagles lose every single game."

"Great." Sandy sounded relieved. "So, what movie are we seeing tonight? I'll call Skye and we can meet at the mall."

"Except . . ." Michelle said slowly, "I kind of promised Matt I'd meet him and the others at the field. I figured I owed it to him as a friend to at least listen to what they had to say."

"Okay. We'll go with you." Sandy whistled softly under her breath. "Wow! Just think of it. One girl and all those guys in the boys' locker room. Gosh, Michelle, it should only happen to me."

CHAPTER 3

The late summer breeze felt good against Michelle's face as she hunched forward on her bike and pedaled along with Sandy and Skye. Most of the other families in their neighborhood were still eating dinner. Here and there, a dog ran across a lawn and barked at them, but mostly it was quiet. She was glad. It gave her a chance to concentrate as she and her friends headed toward the park.

Brian had gone ahead of them, also on his bike. Something about meeting the guys to go over some last-minute details. Michelle figured they wanted to see her kick the ball a few more times to make sure she was consistent. Kind of like a pre-tryout. What they didn't know was that she was checking them out, too. No matter how much they needed her, she might not even want to be part of the Eagles team. Especially now that they wanted her to try out as a boy.

But trying out as a boy wasn't what bothered her the most. Michelle was upset that Skye hadn't been more supportive.

"It's ridiculous! You have no business on the football

field. You're too small," Skye had said.

Probably Michelle should have expected as much from Skye. Until last year, she hadn't had much experience playing competitive sports.

"Stop worrying," Michelle finally told her. "I could fall off my bike and get killed as easily as I could playing football."

"Don't say that!" Skye shuddered. "You better watch out for potholes and popped-up sidewalks. Sandy, you ride first."

But as much as Michelle tried to convince Skye that nothing bad would happen, Skye couldn't believe it. Skye was convinced that if Michelle got hurt, she wouldn't be able to play basketball. And if Michelle didn't play basketball, Skye would have to try out for the team by herself, a fate Skye dreaded. Maybe it was wanting too much to expect Skye to relax.

The sun cast long evening shadows as the girls coasted into the parking lot near the football field. In a line, they headed down the curved path toward Lamar, Rani, and Derek, who were tossing a football back and forth in a slow, easy rhythm. Setting their bikes in a rack beside the snack bar, they wandered over to the edge of the field to watch.

"Where's Matt?" Sandy whispered.

Michelle pointed. "Over by the goalpost talking to Bigmouth. Maybe I better tell them I'm here."

"Wait a sec. I'll go with you."

Leaving Skye, Michelle and Sandy walked across the field. As they came closer, Michelle expected the boys to notice her, but they didn't. Whatever Matt and Brian were talking about had to be pretty serious.

"I don't know, Brian. I think you might be able to tell Michelle is a girl," Matt was saying.

Michelle cleared her throat. From being Brian's sister, she knew how boys talked about girls. Still, it embarrassed her to have heard that much of Matt's conversation—even if it did concern her.

"How?" Brian asked.

"Well, her . . ." Matt blushed, still unaware that Michelle was there.

"Her what?" Brian demanded.

Matt gulped helplessly. "Well, her . . . her . . . her hair, for one thing."

"Don't let that be your problem." Michelle stepped forward. "If I really, *really* wanted to be part of the Eagles football team, I'd simply cut off my hair."

"You will not!" Sandy shrieked. "We'll pin it up if we have to."

"Okay," Michelle said. "But I still didn't say I wanted to be part of the team."

From his hurt expression, Michelle could tell Matt was upset. So could Brian. He punched Matt good-naturedly on the shoulder.

"Trust me," Brian said, cocky as ever. "She's a Dupree. She'll get her drive once she starts kicking the ball. All of us Duprees are competitive. It's part of our DNA."

"I don't know why I'm doing this," Michelle whispered to Sandy as Matt signaled the others to join them at a spot thirty yards from the uprights.

"Hey." Brian slapped Derek on the rump. "Why don't you hold the ball for Michelle and let her kick it for practice. She's still not sure if she can do it."

Michelle glared at Brian. The nerve of her brother!

Couldn't he get anything right? She knew she *could* do it. She just wasn't sure if she *wanted* to do it. She was tired of them automatically thinking of her as one of the guys. She wanted them to think of her as a girl.

"Yeah, everyone knows how important a good kicker is," Derek was saying. "Besides the quarterback, he . . ." Derek stopped to clear his throat. "Sorry, Michelle. *She* might be the most important member of the team."

"Especially in a tight game," Matt added.

They weren't kidding. Lots of times a game depended on whether or not the kicker made the winning field goal.

Michelle waited while Derek knelt down on one knee. He set the ball up and steadied it with his finger. Heart pounding, Michelle lined up a few steps behind the ball. Then, keeping her eyes focused on the ball, she took one short step with her kicking leg and another longer step with her nonkicking leg. She planted her foot next to the pigskin and swung her leg into the ball. It was smooth. It was easy. And while she did it, she thought of nothing else.

Sandy's and Skye's shrieks brought her back to earth.

She kicked two more exactly the same.

"Okay, so she can kick the ball dead on while standing still," Lamar said after her third successful attempt. "How is she going to function in a game situation?"

"Game situation?" At first Michelle was puzzled. "Oh, I get it," she said. "You mean from the snap?"

Matt nodded. "What Lamar means is that it might seem different with the ball coming at you."

"You mean she might panic—like a girl?" Sandy said. "How insulting."

Lamar cocked his head. "That's not what I meant."

28

Hands on her hips, Michelle stepped toe to toe with Lamar. She squinted up at him. He might be big as an ox, but she wasn't frightened. "Maybe you did. Maybe you didn't." She turned to Matt. "Anytime you want to simulate a game play, I'm ready."

It was exactly what Matt wanted to hear. He gestured to his teammates. Rani and Lamar lined up on both sides of him. On a count of three, Matt snapped the ball to Derek, who set the ball in position. Quickly, Michelle went into motion.

Whack! Broing!

Out of the corner of her eye, Michelle saw Lamar leap into the air, trying unsuccessfully to block her kick. She also spotted the ball bouncing on the pole before going between the uprights.

"Good try, Lamar," Matt said.

Lamar smiled sheepishly. "Thanks. For someone so little, Michelle really put the ball up there. I'm impressed."

Derek stood up. "Even so, Michelle's going to need some practice. You have to consider that she's always played indoors on a basketball court. She's never had to contend with wind on a football field."

"Or cold," Brian offered. "Or rain, or snow, or mud."

"Okay, okay," Michelle said. "You make it sound like I'm delivering mail. I get your drift."

"We all see that she can make the extra points," said Rani. "But what about kicking off? Look at her legs. She probably doesn't have enough power to kick the ball deep. I don't want to risk trouble with the coach if she can't do all of it."

Michelle could hardly believe her ears. Rani sounded

29

like he was scrutinizing a thoroughbred before the Kentucky Derby.

"There's always Jocko," Derek cracked.

"No way," Matt said. "I keep telling you, he'd be better at defense. He's too slow to be a good kicker. But Rani's right. We ought to see if Michelle can go the distance."

"Good idea." Brian immediately pulled a kicking tee out of his pocket and began walking downfield. Michelle watched as he put the tee on the ground and set the ball in place. Then, with a grand sweep of his arm, he motioned for her to join him. With his back toward the rest of the guys, he grinned and winked at Michelle.

In that split second, Michelle loved Brian. Not just because he was her brother, but because of the support he showed her. He knew she could kick off. He had confidence in her. He didn't have to say, "C'mon, Sis, you can do it." It was in his heart.

Michelle grinned back at Brian. The ball was in front of her, waiting. And more than a seventh grader, more than a girl, she was an athlete.

Michelle counted seven steps back, placing her farther behind the ball. With her eyes firmly fixed on the football, she ran for it. She swung her leg with the same motion as before. But this time, she connected with the football with more momentum.

"Whoa!" everyone shouted.

"How many miles did that ball fly?" somebody yelled.

"I don't know, but I better find that pigskin before it gets dark," Lamar hollered as he took off in the general direction of Michelle's powerful kick. "If I can't, you've all got to pitch in and buy me a new one."

Meanwhile, Brian, the proud brother, was slapping

everyone on the back like he was the one responsible for Michelle's talent.

Everyone, except Skye, was whooping and hollering like their problems were solved.

"With Michelle in the kicking slot, you guys at least have a chance at beating the Barracudas," Brian said once the others had calmed down. "Otherwise, you're wiped out. Is that what you want?"

"Nope," they agreed.

Even in the dim evening light, Michelle could make out Matt's blush. "So, will you do it, Michelle?" he asked. "Will you try out for the team? You heard your brother. If you don't, we don't stand a chance."

Michelle reached out to touch Matt on the shoulder. "I'll do it."

"And I'm going to help," Sandy bubbled. "I'll take care of her hair. I'm good at that."

"You have to tell me what to expect," Michelle said. "I've seen plenty of games but never a practice. How am I supposed to know what to do?"

"Okay," Matt said enthusiastically. "First, Coach has us warm up with stretching exercises and sprints. After that the big guys work with tackling dummies."

Michelle glanced at Brian and smiled. "I've got plenty of experience with that," she joked.

"Then we usually have some touch games, and after that Coach has us run a few laps," Matt continued. "Since you'll be trying out as kicker, you probably won't have to tackle or play any touch, but you'll have to exercise and run laps."

"That's fine."

"Of course, we can't let anyone else know that you're

trying out." Matt looked directly at Sandy and Skye. "If too many people find out, then it will be too hard to keep the secret. You girls can't tell anyone."

"We won't," Sandy said for both her and Skye.

"Right now only Matt, Lamar, and Rani know," said Brian, "plus Sandy, Skye, me, and Derek. You'll have to keep a lid on this if you're serious about wanting to beat the Barracudas."

"I don't understand," Skye piped up. "What if Coach Brown finds out? Couldn't Michelle get suspended? What about all that tackling? You said Michelle won't have to tackle in practice but what about in a real game? Won't Michelle get hurt?"

"Don't worry," Matt told Skye while looking directly at Michelle. "I'm going to be personally responsible for Michelle. Me, Lamar, and Rani will keep her covered. And while she's working on her kicking, we'll scope out the other guys to see if any of them would have a mean reaction if they did find out."

He fished around in his pocket until he pulled out a folded piece of paper. He handed it to Michelle.

"This is the insurance form your parents have to sign so you can play. You can't try out without it."

Michelle unfolded the form with Skye and Sandy looking over her shoulders. Right away Skye pointed to a line in the middle of the page. "Here, see? You're going to get into major trouble. When you write your name, the coach will automatically know that you're a girl," she said.

Sandy shrugged. "Don't worry. We'll change it," she said brightly. "This is going to be really cool!"

"Change it? To what?" Michelle asked.

"How about Mike?" Brian teased.

"It can't be Smidge," Matt muttered. "Everyone knows Smidge from the basketball team. Maybe we could use Mike, if Michelle doesn't mind."

Michelle shook her head. "No, my mom would never sign that. She always says one son is plenty."

"I know," Sandy said smartly. "How about if she signs the paper as Michelle. After that I'll put a 't' in and take an 'e' out. I'll change her name to Mitchell."

"Mitchell?" Michelle spluttered.

Skye sounded absolutely amazed. "F-f-forgery?"

"It's not f-f-forgery," Sandy mimicked. "I'm not signing Mrs. Dupree's name. We all know that wouldn't be right. I'm only changing Michelle's. You could say I'm using some inventive spelling. Michelle, Smidge, Mitchell. What difference does it make how it's spelled? It's the same person. Right, Michelle?"

Michelle let out a deep breath, unsure what she'd gotten herself into.

"Yeah, right," she mumbled mostly to herself as she slowly shook her head and looked toward the heavens.

CHAPTER 4

Hercules met Michelle and Brian at the kitchen door.

"Thanks, Herc." Michelle patted his head while taking a grimy sock from the dog's mouth. "Good job, fella." She smiled mischievously at Brian before tossing the sock over her shoulder and into his face. If Brian's mouth had been open as usual, the sock would have gone right in. Too bad!

"That was unnecessary, young lady." Mrs. Dupree stopped stirring and poured two glasses of iced tea from the pitcher. Judging by her mother's damp hair and shiny running shorts, she had just returned from jogging while exercising Hercules, something her parents did almost every night. It wasn't exactly a good time to clown around.

"Sorry, Brian."

"Yeah, well, okay. Don't let it happen again."

Behind her mother's back, Michelle stuck out her tongue.

"Nice, Michelle." Brian turned to their mother. "Wow,

you really worked up a good sweat, Mom." He took the glass of tea intended for their father.

Michelle rolled her eyes, amazed at how Brian always managed to say the most unflattering things to girls without even realizing it. If, miracle of miracles, he ever had a girlfriend, that girl would be plain out of luck.

Michelle eased the team's insurance form out of her pocket. She waited until her mother finished taking a long sip of iced tea before sliding the paper across the counter. "You have to sign this tonight."

"Yeah, she needs it for tomorrow's practice," Brian added. "You know how Michelle played basketball with the boys last year because of the budget cuts. Well, they're still cutting the budget. Now she wants to play football."

"Hmmm, interesting." Mrs. Dupree's forehead wrinkled as she glanced first at Brian and then at Michelle. "Michelle, how about getting me another glass for your father?"

Carrying the folded sheet of paper into the living room along with the drinks, Mrs. Dupree collapsed on the couch beside her husband. She read the form, then eyed Brian suspiciously. "Why, Brian, I'm impressed."

"Why?" Brian looked surprised.

"You certainly have come a long way in a year's time." She turned to her husband, who was fanning himself with a magazine while drinking his tea. "Darling, Michelle wants to try out for the football team."

Mr. Dupree stopped fanning. "What?"

"Yes, and it appears that our son is behind her one hundred percent. Isn't that remarkable?"

"I don't know about remarkable. Certainly unexpected."

"Especially since last year he was so adamantly opposed to Michelle's joining the boys' basketball team. Brian, you have made such strides!"

Michelle held her breath. Surely Brian would be able to tell that their mother, while singing her flowery praises, was smelling a rat.

"Mom, that was different," he said.

"How?" their dad asked.

"Well, for one thing, I was going to the same school as Michelle. And the other is that now I'm a lot more mature in my thinking. Besides that, we all know that Michelle is a great jock. She proved that when she played basketball with the guys. So if she wants to play football . . ."

Mr. Dupree set his empty glass down on the table with a thud. "I never heard her talk about playing football. That's a brutal sport."

Mrs. Dupree stood up. "We let Brian play."

"That's different."

"How?"

"He's a boy," Mr. Dupree said, apparently without thinking.

Bristling, Mrs. Dupree arched one eyebrow. "Well, I will admit that football might be a bit more aggressive than basketball. However—"

"Mom, Dad, we only play eight games," Michelle interrupted.

"Eight?" Brian said. "Last year we played six."

Michelle grinned. "I was counting the play-off and the championship."

Mrs. Dupree smiled. "That's my girl. Always thinking positively."

"Anyway, Dad," Michelle argued, "I'm only trying out

as a kicker. Kickers never get hurt. They don't have to tackle or do any of the heavy stuff. They don't even get to join in the huddle. You guys won't even have to spend any extra money on equipment like you did for Brian. First of all, I won't need a steel-fortified, heavy-duty, gold-medal, athletic-supporting jockstrap."

Immediately, Mr. Dupree and Brian turned beet red and started to sputter.

"And don't forget, you let me play basketball with the guys," Michelle went on. "So what's the difference . . . as long as I keep my grades up?"

"Well, I have to agree that kicking an occasional extra point may not be the most dangerous athletic activity," Mr. Dupree said, once he'd recovered from her reference to male-only sports underwear. "But it seems to me that once Michelle makes the team as kicker, she'll be called upon to perform a few extra duties as well."

Michelle frowned. "Like what?" Coach Brown wouldn't make her carry the water bucket, would he?

"Like kickoffs and punting. Either occasion would put you in the thick of things. The punter is usually the last player down the field. There's a good chance you'd get knocked down by the opposing defense if a punt returner broke a long run."

"In that league?" Brian said. "Oh, Dad, that's rare."

Brian glanced nervously at Michelle. Their mother was reading the section on the form about the team doctor. Michelle nodded. She and Brian were on the same wavelength. A team doctor could ruin everything.

Michelle tugged her mom's sleeve. "Mom?" she squeaked. "You're not going to say I have to see the team doctor, are you?"

Mrs. Dupree glanced up, surprised. "Sweetie, I believe it's required."

"No, Mom. If you look down at the bottom, it says that, if you prefer, you can see the doctor of your choice. Well, um, I've been meaning to tell you that I think it's time I saw . . ." Michelle rolled her eyes while jerking her head in Brian's direction. She hoped her mother took the hint. "What I mean is, I'd rather see a lady doctor."

"Oh." Mrs. Dupree straightened. She brushed Michelle's hair off her forehead. "Why, sweetie, of course."

Mr. Dupree glanced from his wife to his daughter, a concerned look on his face. "Is there something I missed?"

"No, darling. It seems our Michelle is growing up. She's ready to see a lady doctor."

Brian strutted around behind Michelle. "Of course she's growing up. She even wears one of those Spandex, anti-bounce, keep-them-in-place sports bras," he said, snapping one of her straps for emphasis.

"Ouch!" Michelle yelped. "Cut that out!"

"Guys, enough!" Mrs. Dupree exclaimed. Quickly, she bent over and signed the form, just as Michelle had hoped she would.

"Hey, Sis. You did pretty good," Brian said once he and Michelle got upstairs. "Mom really bought all that stuff about needing to see a lady doctor. Kind of makes you wonder, doesn't it? I mean, they're supposed to be the smart ones." He handed her a helmet and a pair of shoes he'd outgrown. "I've got other helmets and cleats if these don't fit."

"Thanks. If you have some shoulder pads, that would make it a little easier for me to fool the coach."

Michelle put the helmet on. She folded her arms across her chest and watched Brian rummage around in his closet. Looking through the thick bars of the face mask gave her a sudden feeling of power. Unfortunately, it didn't last long.

"Shoulder pads, no prob. But it's going to take more than a helmet, shoes, and shoulder pads to make you look like a guy. It's the subtle things, you know?"

Michelle frowned. She didn't know.

"You don't exactly walk like a guy." Brian flipped a football in the air, end over end, and caught it. "And there are a couple of other things that guys do that you ought to know or you're not going to fit in."

"What are you talking about?"

She waited while he sauntered across the room and sat down on his bed.

"Guys spit, Michelle," he said. "Once in a while, you've got to spit. And not some sissy spit. You've got to really put one out there. Guys don't say it, but they kind of size each other up by how they spit."

"That's ridiculous."

"Suit yourself. That's not all. Like I told you before, you don't exactly walk like a guy."

"Okay, so how do guys walk?"

Brian stood up. He tilted his head back. He jutted out his chin and did something to his pecs to make them pop. "Watch the knees," he instructed Michelle. "And pay real close attention to the elbows."

"Elbows? Knees?" Michelle said. "I can't just walk?"

"Shut up and watch, twerp. I'm doing you a favor."

Michelle took a deep breath. Meanwhile, Brian bent his knees slightly and curved his muscular arms away

39

from his body, as if he were cradling the whole heavy world in them. Then he swaggered, toes out, across the room.

Michelle wrinkled her nose. "I'm not sure I can do that." At the same time she wondered why she would ever want to. Then she remembered. Coach Brown didn't want girls on his team.

"It takes practice but it's a little easier when you have your shoulder pads on," Brian admitted. He strutted back toward Michelle. "When you get really good at it, you can walk and spit at the same time."

Michelle was stunned. No wonder Brian's grades were so bad. He spent all of his energy studying the wrong things.

"Of course, you've got to remember to raise your helmet," Brian said, still talking about the fine art of spitting. "You wouldn't want to hit the bars on your face mask and have your spit come right back at you. Now you try it."

Michelle let Brian help her tilt her head until it was at the right angle. "This is pretty uncomfortable," she complained.

"You'll get used to it. Now let's see how you walk."

With her head tilted awkwardly, Michelle tried swaggering across the room. "How do you see where you're going?"

Brian shrugged. "Well, sometimes you don't. Why do you think guys trip all the time?"

"Big feet?"

Brian groaned. "That's not all. I saved the best for last."

Michelle took the helmet off and brushed her bangs back into place. "I'm holding my breath."

Brian closed one eye while watching her intently with the other. "Guys scratch," he said.

Michelle shook her head. "No, Brian. *You* scratch."

"No, Michelle," Brian mimicked. "I'm just the only guy you caught scratching. That's because guys don't scratch around girls. That would be crude. But when it's only guys together, we scratch all over the place."

Brian leaned closer and lowered his voice. "I'm telling you this because I don't want you to be so shocked that when some football comes sailing out of the sky, you let it conk you on the head and knock you unconscious."

Talk about shock. Michelle didn't know what to think.

Brian wasn't finished. He leaned back against the headboard of his bed and pulled a Nerf football from under his pillow and tossed it at the ceiling. "I don't know why we do it, unless it's because it feels good. But guys scratch. We always have. If you don't believe me, ask Dad."

Michelle stepped back, unsure. "I don't think so."

"Okay, suit yourself," he said. "But take it from me, little sister. If you're not scratching away like the rest of the guys, they're going to know right off that you're not one of them. So if you get yourself in a tight situation and it looks like one of the guys might be thinking that you're trying to pull something on them, all you have to do is pick a spot, any spot, and scratch like crazy. Because that's what guys do."

Michelle left Brian's room carrying her helmet, shoulder pads, and cleats. It was a lot to ponder.

"Don't make me wait. Let me see your nails." That was the first thing Sandy said the next morning when she saw Michelle. "Oh, poor baby," was the second thing.

Mr. and Mrs. Dupree had already left for work, and Brian was at an early-bird football practice at the high school. According to plan, Sandy was supposed to help Michelle with her new disguise as Mitchell.

"Honestly, I didn't believe you on the phone last night when you said you filed them down," Sandy said, still babbling on about the tragic demise of Michelle's fingernails. "And you removed your polish!" she shrieked. "Honestly, Michelle, without your nails you are practically naked."

Michelle stared briefly at the hands where beautiful, carefully cultivated, female fingernails once grew. Now there were just little chips of nothingness.

"It wasn't like I had a choice," she whimpered. "Mauve Allure would have been a dead giveaway."

"Yeah," Sandy agreed. "Mitchell would never wear Mauve Allure. So what do we do first? The permission form?"

Sandy sat down at Michelle's desk. In less than a minute "Michelle" was changed to "Mitchell."

"Next is your hair," Sandy said, leading Michelle into the bathroom. "I have everything here in this little bag from the House of Pretty. Elastic bands, masking tape. I didn't bother to bring gel since you said we could use Brian's."

She opened the medicine cabinet and grabbed a container of gel, but Michelle wasn't paying attention. "You're going to tape my hair?" she squeaked.

Sandy turned around. "Of course," she said matter-of-factly. "How else do you think we're going to get it to stay up and be invisible?" She fluffed Michelle's bangs and examined the tendrils that curled beside each ear. "Don't worry. It won't hurt a bit. Your hair is in expert hands."

Michelle gulped. Not a reassuring thought. "Those expert hands once turned my hair green."

Sandy made a disgusted clicking sound. "Will you never forget?" She motioned Michelle to sit down on the toilet seat. "That was in kindergarten."

"It was green until third grade."

Sandy started to giggle. "Was not, silly. Your mother got the finger paints out the very next day with egg whites and cornmeal or something equally gross and homemade." She swept Michelle's hair up off her shoulders. "Brian's gel shouldn't feel all that bad."

Michelle closed her eyes and held her breath as Sandy pumped a good six inches of cold slime into her hair.

"This is unbelievable," Sandy marveled as she oozed the gel from Michelle's hairline to the ends of each strand. "You almost smell like Brian."

Michelle might have barfed, except that Sandy had started ripping masking tape off the roll. She was cutting the masking tape in long strips and sticking them to the vanity.

"What in the world are you doing?" Michelle reached back and tried to feel her hair.

"Don't touch!" Sandy swatted her fingers as she banded Michelle's hair into a long gooky ponytail. "I'm giving you a head wrap. People go to salons and pay for this service. I'm doing it for free."

With that, she smeared more gel around Michelle's ears. It was too scary. Sandy was laying masking tape along her hairline.

"Whatever you do, don't cover my ears," Michelle wailed. "I have to hear the audibles."

"The what-ibles?"

"Audibles," Michelle explained as Sandy began crisscrossing the masking tape over the rest of her head. "That's when the quarterback calls the plays telling everyone what to do. You know. *Sixteen, thirty-four. Hup. Hup. Hup.*"

A few minutes later Michelle was staring in the mirror at a gigantic tan hornet's nest, while behind her Sandy proudly surveyed her masterpiece.

"There. That will work." Sandy touched the swollen globe of masking tape that used to be Michelle's head. "Now your helmet will fit good and snug. You won't have to worry about your hair slipping out. You won't have to cut it either. Honestly, Michelle, that would be the worst."

"No," Michelle said apprehensively. "The worst is going to be getting this head wrap *un*wrapped. How are we going to do that?"

"Oh!" Sandy stepped back and blinked in surprise. "Honestly, Michelle. You don't know how lucky you are. After your practice, you're going to get a hydroxy peel. Don't raise your eyebrows at me. You won't be using harmful acid or chemicals," Sandy said as she turned to rinse the smelly gel off her hands. "You'll be using super water jets sprayed from the nifty new Savvy Salon Shower Attachment that my mother ordered from Shoppers Network on TV. It just came in the mail yesterday." Sandy pulled open the shower curtain. "All we have to do is hook it over your showerhead. We don't even need to call a plumber."

Michelle gulped. "Are you sure about this?"

"Absolutely. Your head wrap will fall apart like a soggy newspaper without the ink. Then all we have to do is wad up the whole mess and throw it in a plastic bag. I have everything organized in my tote bag."

Michelle sighed, fully resigned to her fate. "Let's hope this works," she said, crossing her fingers in Sandy's smiling face. "I'm supposed to call my dad at the store so he can drive us to practice."

"With your helmet on, you really look cool," Sandy told Michelle as they sat on the front porch, waiting for Mr. Dupree. "Take it from an expert. You could fool me."

"Check it out." Michelle dusted off her pants and took a few steps down the sidewalk. She held her helmet-laden head at an awkward angle while concentrating on keeping her toes out, knees and elbows slightly bent. To help, she tried thinking of Arnold Schwarzenegger.

"Wow! I'm so impressed," Sandy said softly. "You even walk like a boy."

"Big hero Brian showed me last night." It was only for Sandy's benefit that Michelle decided not to spit. And since Sandy was a girl, she didn't scratch either.

"There's only one problem," Sandy said suddenly. "You don't sound like a boy."

Michelle stopped dead in her tracks. "I don't?" She lifted her helmet slightly so she could get a good view of Sandy without the face mask. "Brian didn't say anything about my voice."

Sandy shrugged. "Maybe he's so busy talking himself, he never paid any attention to how guys sound. But I do."

As far as Michelle could remember, Sandy's comment was the closest she had ever come to admitting that Brian had a big mouth. "Terrific," she mumbled under her breath. After all this trouble getting her head gelled and taped, Coach Brown would find out the truth as soon as she opened her mouth.

"Most of the guys have lower voices than us girls." Sandy stopped for a moment to think. "Well, some guys start out low and then their voice kind of squeaks before it turns low again. But you still have to say that their voices are lower than ours."

Michelle flopped down on the porch step beside Sandy. "Maybe I could be the one person on the team who never opens her—oops, I mean *his*—mouth."

Sandy shook her head. "Mission impossible! You've got to lower your voice. The only thing that might work, short of surgery on your vocal cords, is if you pretend you have a mouth full of gravel."

Terrific, Michelle thought as her father beeped the horn. If she made the team, she'd have to memorize the Eagles' game plans and practice several kicking techniques. Now, thanks to Brian and Sandy, she had to learn a whole new way of walking and talking, spitting and scratching. Playing football for the Eagles was going to be harder than she'd ever imagined.

CHAPTER 5

"Gosh, Michelle. You look great," Matt said softly as he swung the gate open to the athletic field. Rivers of sweat ran down both sides of his face. He pulled at the neck of his oversized T-shirt with one hand to mop up the sweat while holding his helmet with the other. Michelle, of course, was wearing her helmet.

"Doesn't she?" Sandy bounced on her toes, excited to be part of the intrigue. "This is going to be so much fun." Sandy stopped abruptly. "We probably ought to get used to calling her by her football name. Right, Mitchell?"

Inside the boiling hot helmet, Michelle's eyes narrowed into slits. She was going to hate being called Mitchell.

"Right, Mitchell?" Sandy said again.

Matt's eyebrows rose with concern. "Are you okay, Michelle? Er, Mitchell?" he asked as Sandy gave him a poke in the ribs.

"Yeah, fine." Michelle tried to smile.

Satisfied, Sandy spun around and whipped out her notebook and the purple clicky pen that perfectly matched her sneakers and stretchy ponytail holder. "See you kids later," she called over her shoulder, clicking her pen excitedly as she hurried toward a group of boys beside the water station.

Michelle turned to Matt. "C'mon. Let's go find the coach and get this over with."

Since it was the last day of tryouts, none of the other kids paid much attention as they walked across the field toward a tall, tanned man in blue shorts and a yellow T-shirt.

"Coach?" Matt said.

When he turned around, the second thing Michelle noticed was the word COACH written in big letters across his shirt. The first thing she had noticed was that he was handsomer than she'd expected, and younger, too—lots younger. He didn't even have a belly yet. One look at Coach Brown, and Sandy would swoon herself into a frenzy. If Michelle didn't know better, she'd say he was tennis champion Pete Sampras's twin brother.

"Coach Brown, this is the kid I was telling you about," Matt said. "I think we could really use Mich . . . er . . . Mitchell in the kicking department."

Michelle eyed the tanned face of the man who would decide her fate, hoping that he didn't catch Matt's slip. He didn't. Instead, he lifted his baseball cap and wiped the sweat off his forehead with the back of his hand. She waited while he combed his curly black hair with his long fingers before adjusting the brim and settling the cap back on his head where it belonged.

"Mitchell! That's a nerd name," he said.

Michelle couldn't believe her ears. What kind of insulting comment was that?

Matt had warned her that Coach Brown wasn't like Coach Hawkins, who had coached them in basketball. He wasn't kidding. Coach Hawkins wasn't handsome, but he was nice. He was fair, too.

Coach Brown wasn't finished. "Mitchell. The name's bigger than you are. I hope you're not wasting my time."

Michelle tensed at the reference to her size. It took every ounce of resolve to keep her mouth shut, but until she mastered a gravelly voice, she couldn't take the chance.

Just then Lamar ambled over. He had on his cleats and was carrying a helmet. "Yo, Mitch. Glad you could make it."

Michelle jumped as Lamar slapped her on the rump. She glared daggers at him from behind her face mask, but if Lamar cared, he didn't let on. He was too busy talking to the coach. "How about if I hold the ball so Mitch can show you what he's got."

"Good idea." Coach Brown pointed his finger at Matt. "And I want you to work on your fakes. During that last series you were dancing around like Madame Fufu in a pink tutu. Sometimes knowing how to fake a pass is as important as knowing how to throw one. Playing quarterback takes acting ability. You've got to bluff the opposition."

"Yes, sir." Matt didn't crack a smile. "I already left some balls out there in the center for Mitch."

Coach Brown nodded. "Good thinking, Peterson."

"Listen, we might want the coach and the others to see me as a guy, but you and I know that I'm not," Michelle told Lamar as they started toward the center of the playing field.

"Yeah. So?"

"So you can keep your grubby hands to yourself."

Laughing, Lamar threw his hands in the air. "Hey, what did I do?"

Michelle glared at him so hard she thought the metal bars on her face mask might melt. "You know perfectly well what you did. You slapped my butt."

"Hey, I was trying to be convincing."

"Well, I don't buy that phony excuse. So remember, hands off."

"Sorry. I guess I got carried away."

"One more time and *you'll* be the one carried away. C'mon, let's see if I can wallop that pigskin as good as ever."

A couple of minutes later footballs were sailing between the uprights just as they had the night before. Each time Lamar glanced over to be certain the coach had seen. Then he gave her the A-OK sign. "Way to go, Mitch."

Finally, Coach Brown shouted, "That's fine. Let's see what Shorty can do from farther away."

Whoa! Michelle scooped up a ball and trotted after Lamar toward midfield, being careful to keep her head down.

"Farther. I can still see you," Coach shouted.

"Geez, what is this?" Lamar grumbled as they left the thirty-five, passed the forty-five, and headed toward the fifty.

A loud blast of the coach's whistle stopped them.

"That's the killing spot right there," Coach Brown bellowed. "Pressure's on, Mitch-*ell*," he shouted, poking fun at her new name. "Put your foot to it. Let's see it fly."

Lamar knelt on the ground and pulled a kicking tee out of his pocket. He began feeling around for a level place.

Michelle took a deep breath. It was getting hot. Where they were standing, there was no shade and very little breeze. Out of the corner of her eye, she couldn't help but notice Sandy hanging around the water station, practicing for her sports reporter position by asking questions and writing everything in a notebook. What a trouper! No one would ever suspect that the real reason she was there was to give a certain Michelle Dupree a healthy dose of moral support.

At the same time, Michelle made another important observation. Despite what Brian had told her, none of the guys appeared to be scratching. Once in a while Coach Brown would lift up his baseball cap to scratch his head, or he'd rub his chest. Still, it wasn't nearly the scratch-fest Brian had described. Maybe, Michelle thought, it was because of Sandy. Brian did say guys wouldn't scratch much if a girl was around.

"Hey," Lamar snapped. "Are we going to stand around casting shadows all day or are you going to kick this ball?"

Just like before, Michelle counted seven steps from the ball. She turned around, ran forward, and swung her leg with her instep planted in the middle of the pigskin. The ball went soaring.

Lamar let out a loud whoop as he raced off to fetch the ball. Michelle grinned—but not for long.

"Not bad," Coach Brown bellowed. "Was that half a tank of gas, Half Pint? Next kick, show me the high octane." He wrote something on his clipboard.

Michelle stared at Coach Brown. When he looked up from the clipboard, he stared hard at her. Afraid that he might recognize her as a girl, Michelle quickly bent her

51

head back down and began tapping the ground with her foot. She was still shuffling around when from somewhere in the background she heard a faint shout.

"Hey, Mitch! Heads up."

Along the sideline, Sandy was frantically waving her arms while jumping up and down. Michelle frowned. Leave it to Sandy to change her mind. She'd already given up on being a reporter. Now she was trying out for cheerleading. But something told Michelle to look closer. She squinted at Sandy. She was pointing up in the air.

Michelle turned around and gazed up to where Sandy was pointing. It was a good thing she did. A second later, the football would have conked her in the head, knocking her unconscious. Instead, Michelle snatched it and, in one fluid motion, brought it to her chest and ran it into the end zone.

Matt was there waiting.

"Way to go, Mitch," Matt said under his breath, his brown eyes twinkling.

There was no time to respond. Behind her the coach was hollering. "Good hustle. Great reflexes. But let's hope you never have to run that pattern. A big defensive tackle would flatten you like a pancake."

Michelle grinned at Matt so wide that even under the shadow of her helmet he couldn't miss it. Until she'd put the ball between the uprights on Jefferson's big field, until she'd kicked it downfield to the ten yard line, she hadn't cared if she'd made the team. Now, suddenly, she did. And if she was reading Coach Brown right, it sounded to her like she'd made it.

Whooo-eee!

"Okay, team." Coach whistled, signaling for everyone

to join him in a big circle. "It's important that we get off on the right foot at tomorrow's practice. It'll be our first practice as the official Jefferson Eagles, and I want it to run smooth as silk."

He held his arm out and tapped his watch. "Four o'clock. I want you here on the field ready to stretch out and play hard. That shouldn't be a problem. School is dismissed at three. That gives you an hour to get your practice uniforms and equipment out of the locker room, change, and be here on the field ready to go. Got that, men?"

The boys roared their acceptance. "Yes, sir!"

Only Michelle was horrified. Sitting on the bleachers, Sandy must have been thinking the same incredible thing. Her hands covered her mouth. Her face had paled. Her eyes were as wide as saucers.

Matt, Lamar, Rani, Derek, and Michelle's ever-loving brother, Brian, had never told them. They'd never planned on Michelle changing her clothes in the boys' locker room.

CHAPTER 6

"**M**om!" Brian shouted from the top of the stairs. He had a towel wrapped around his middle. His hair was still wet from his shower. So was the bathroom floor.

"Did you do the laundry? Where are my socks?" he hollered, panic-stricken. "You don't expect me to wear used ones on the first day of high school, do you?"

"The basket is on the landing," Mrs. Dupree called from downstairs. "Michelle, it was your turn to fold the laundry. Did you do as I asked?"

"Yesterday," Michelle shouted back.

"Did you see any of Brian's socks?"

"No, I didn't."

"Brian, your socks never made it into the laundry. It's your own fault. You're starting high school today. The least you can do is take care of your own socks. Go grab a pair of your dad's from his dresser drawer."

Knowing that Brian would make a mess of the bathroom as usual, Michelle had risen early to use it first. Even though her bus came later than Brian's, she'd already dressed and eaten breakfast. She was in front of her mirror inspecting her new denim jumper while fixing her hair for the millionth time when she heard Brian set out on his great sock search. Hercules, curled in a ball on her bed, looked very disturbed. Meanwhile, Michelle covered her mouth to keep from laughing out loud as Brian went ballistic.

"Dad's socks? Are you crazy? He wears that skinny brown kind with the little green foxes on them. The kids will think I'm weird."

Brian stomped over to the landing and began emptying the laundry basket on the floor. "Where are my socks? It's a conspiracy. I can't *find* my socks."

In a flash Hercules bolted off the bed, a shimmering blur of gold. Nose to floor, he raced past Michelle and down the stairs, only to return a few minutes later, the proud bearer of a pair of stiff white socks, which he laid at Brian's feet.

"Woof!" the big dog barked. *"Woof!"*

The stunned expression on Brian's face almost cracked Michelle up.

She waited until Brian left for school before hauling her football gear to the garage. Wearing it was a lot easier than carrying it, she soon found out. The bulky shoulder pads kept knocking into doorways. On her way down the steps, the cleats banged against her knees. And when she tried to juggle everything in her arms, she only managed to drop her helmet.

Her arms loaded, Michelle staggered into the kitchen. "Mom, I'm putting my football equipment and stuff in your car."

She hoped she wouldn't bang into the kitchen table,

where her mom sat reading the morning paper and drinking coffee.

Mrs. Dupree must have been thinking the same thing. Quickly, she jumped up, pushed her chair in, and removed the coffee cup from the table. "Let me help you, sweetie." She eased the shoestrings from around Michelle's fingers and took the cleats. She took the helmet, too.

Michelle smiled. "Thanks, Mom." They put everything in the backseat. "Don't forget, I'm coming to the shop after school and I'll need my gear. Can you have Dad put it in the bathroom for me so it will be ready? I won't have much time."

"Will do. Are you sure you don't need one of us to pick you up after practice?"

Michelle shook her head. "No, that's okay. Matt and his mom are giving me a ride." She grabbed her knapsack. "I better hurry. Sandy's probably already at the bus stop."

"That's one way of avoiding the boys' locker room," Sandy said when Michelle told her Brian's solution for changing into her football uniform. "But how are you supposed to get your official jersey and matching Spandex pants? All you have is your shoulder covers."

"Not shoulder covers—pads," Michelle said. "We don't know yet. Matt's trying to figure something out."

"Oh." Sandy swung her backpack over her shoulder as the bus pulled up in front of the school. "Well, I'd be happy to break into the boys' locker room for you, except I don't want to be expelled on the first day of school."

"Right." Michelle laughed and scrambled out of her seat as the bus opened its doors in front of Jefferson Junior High. Michelle and Sandy headed toward the entrance and stepped into the current of bodies moving into the building. Twice Michelle jumped up so she could see. Once she thought she recognized someone she hadn't seen since before vacation. More than once, she heard her name called out, but there was no chance to turn around.

It wasn't until they were inside the building and everyone started splitting up and going in different directions that Michelle was finally able to catch her breath.

"The first day is always the hardest," she said to Sandy as they leaned against the wall across from the office.

"I remember." Sandy nodded toward a perky cheerleader in her blue-and-gold uniform. She was standing under the clock in front of a group of helpless-looking kids. "Sixth graders," Sandy whispered to Michelle. "They look like lost little babies. Do you think we were ever like that?"

Michelle grimaced. "Not a chance."

The bell rang, and the girls headed their separate ways. Michelle wouldn't see Sandy again until Teen Living, their last class before lunch.

By eleven-twenty, Michelle still hadn't seen Matt. She and Matt should have compared schedules on the phone. The day was almost half over and she still didn't have the slightest idea how she was supposed to get her football uniform without crashing the boys' locker room.

Everything was too confusing. How was she

supposed to concentrate? Her math teacher wanted college rule paper. Her English teacher wanted wide rule. Or was her English teacher talking about college?

Matt had told her not to worry, he'd take care of everything. Then where was he? Was he even in school? Michelle hadn't seen Rani or Lamar either.

She was hoping Sandy would know something as she hurried through the corridors toward the technology wing. She remembered the Teen Living classrooms from orientation. They were actually two classrooms separated by a folding partition. One half had sewing machines set up on little tables with wire mannequins propped in the corner. The other half resembled a kitchen, only with lots more appliances, counter space, and wooden stools.

When Michelle entered, both sections were already packed with kids. She squeezed into a spot between Sandy and Skye.

"Check out the guys. Wow! This is Teen Living for real," Sandy gushed, batting her eyes for emphasis. "I saw Matt a minute ago."

"You did? Where?" Michelle gasped. "I need to talk to him right away."

"That's what I told him. I said, 'Michelle told me to tell you that you have to tell her—'"

"I didn't tell you to tell him anything," Michelle butted in.

Sandy looked hurt. "But I thought you'd want me to. Didn't you?"

Just then a young woman with curly blond hair entered the room. She was wearing slim white slacks and a purple blouse with a lacy camisole peeking through the V neckline. The boys straightened up fast.

"G' morning, y'all," she drawled sweetly as she took a clipboard off the counter. "My name is Miss Ashley Ashleigh and I'll be teaching the cooking curriculum. Mrs. Ross, that lady over yonder with the tape measure around her neck, will be teaching you sewing. Now let's see if we can't get y'all where you belong and get these classes moving."

Since most lists started alphabetically in descending order, Miss Ashleigh said she'd read hers in ascending order.

"Right on," Sandy Vacaro cheered along with Lamar Washington.

"As your names are called for cooking, I'd like y'all to move toward the cupboards."

"Oh, good, I get to sew first," Sandy said a few minutes later. "I'm glad. I cook enough at home, and I already know how to run a dishwasher. I'll probably sew something for Homecoming—in case I get asked."

"We don't have a Homecoming game. That's in high school," Skye whispered.

"Oh, well, I'll sew something for high school then. I wonder if we're allowed to use sequins."

Skye tapped Michelle on the shoulder and grinned. She and Michelle had been assigned to cooking along with Matt. "This is going to be so neat. We'll have to do our projects together," she said as Miss Ashleigh waved them into the big kitchen.

Michelle craned her neck to search for Matt and was relieved to find him standing beside a cooktop. Now if she could only weave her way through the crowd. Behind them she heard the partition slide across the tracks.

Judging by the teacher's drawl and appearance, she was going to be a real softie. That meant getting a message to Matt would be a cinch. Already some of the boys were using the measuring spoons to flick M&Ms at the girls. But what was that delicious smell?

"It smells like cookies," Michelle said as she and Skye edged closer to Matt.

"I think you might be hallucinating," Skye whispered back.

Michelle took another sniff. "It can't be from the cafeteria. That's on the other side of the building. Besides, they never fix anything good like cookies."

"That's exactly why I bring my lunch. You can't be too careful."

"And that is exactly why y'all are here in Teen Living." When Miss Ashleigh winked and smiled directly at Skye, Skye blushed. "In this unit y'all are going to learn so much about proper food preparation." With that she swung open a cabinet door and pulled out a heaping tray of freshly baked chocolate chip cookies.

"All right!" the boys shouted.

At the same time, Michelle caught Matt's eye. Quickly, she tapped her watch with her finger and mouthed, "We need to talk."

Matt nodded and sent a large plastic bowl of measuring cups and spoons off the counter and clattering to the floor. When he ducked behind the cooktop to gather the spoons and cups, Michelle ducked, too.

"I figured out how to handle this afternoon," Matt whispered as they dropped spoons and cups back into the bowl. "Don't worry about the locker room. I'll get your stuff and meet you."

"Where?"

"At the back door by the gym. Give me a few minutes. I'll be there by five after three."

"Good. I'm changing at my folks' store." She started to tell him how that was Brian's idea, but she didn't have the chance. Miss Ashleigh had bent down between them.

"Y'all don't want any of my cookies?"

"Yes, ma'am. Thank you." Matt blushed as he lifted a cookie off the tray.

Michelle took a deep breath of relief. Any other teacher would have sent her and Matt marching off to the principal's office—exactly what they did not need.

"You should have seen the boys in cooking class. They were so clumsy!" Skye shrieked in the cafeteria. At the next table, all the boys were staring. "They didn't even know how to hold a potholder. They shouldn't even be there. Cooking is for girls. Boys shouldn't be allowed."

Sandy grunted. "Girls belong here. Boys belong there. You sound like Michelle's Coach Macho Man. Yech."

"Shhh!" Michelle jabbed Sandy. "Watch it. Someone will hear you."

Sandy grimaced. "Sorry."

Michelle nodded. "Well, I definitely think guys should learn how to do their own laundry and cook and stuff. But instead of Teen Living they should call it Survival Skills."

"Oh, I almost forgot to tell you," Sandy said, changing the subject. "I stopped by to see Ms. Cramer. She's the sponsor for *The Lantern* this year. Guess what? It's official. It's my job to cover the games. I get a press pass and everything. That means I get in free!" Sandy added in case no one else understood.

Skye began carefully peeling her banana. "Can I still go with you? Where are you going to sit? Are you going to sit with other reporters?" she asked.

"I probably get to sit anywhere I want. Maybe with Channel Nine News, or Apple Cable. Isn't this too cool? We'll still go together," she reassured Skye. "If anyone asks, I'll say you're my assistant and you can sit with me. I'll even let you carry my new clicky pen."

"Hi, guys."

Michelle looked up as two of Sandy's friends from the Pep Squad pulled out chairs and joined them at the table. "Did I hear you say you were going to the game?"

"Skye and I are," Sandy chirped. "We'll be working *all* the games."

"What about you?" The girls were staring at Michelle.

Michelle opened her carton of milk and took a sip with her straw. "I'm not exactly sure," she said. "Probably not. I might have to help my folks at our store."

"Too bad!" the girl next to Skye said.

"Tell them it's our first game," the other suggested.

"Yeah. The first game is so important. You need to show your school spirit. That's what junior high is all about. Besides, the boys need all the help they can get."

Michelle glanced at Skye and Sandy. Any other time they would have come to her defense. But this time that would have meant big trouble.

CHAPTER 7

"**P**ssst, Michelle. Over here." Matt's voice came from the bushes near the parking lot behind the gymnasium. "I've got your uniform."

Michelle breathed a sigh of relief. "I was looking all over for you. When you weren't by the door, I thought you'd been caught. That would've been disaster city!" she exclaimed.

"Sorry. I didn't want anyone to see me with an extra set of clothes and a helmet and start asking questions." He dumped a bundle of blue and gold into her arms and plopped an Eagles helmet on top. "I hope everything is the right size. I remembered last year you said you wore size Smidge." He grinned at the joke. "I figured you must have grown some since then."

What a nice thing to say. When it came to compliments, Matt had it all over Brian.

"What excuse did you finally give your mom about the rest of your gear?" he asked.

"Oh, I told her I didn't want it smelling up my locker the first day of school." Michelle opened up her knapsack and pulled out a black plastic trash bag. She stuffed the helmet and team practice uniform in the bag. "My mom thinks the reason I'm supplying my own gear is because of the budget cuts. I didn't exactly tell her that. She kind of made it up herself."

Matt smiled like he understood. "You know everyone on the team has his own locker in the locker room. Goofy Jocko already stuck a Power Rangers decal on his. We'll have to figure a way so Coach doesn't notice that you're not using your locker."

Michelle turned to leave.

"Make it snappy," Matt called after her. "Coach will kill you if you're late."

Michelle hurried down the hill toward her parents' shop with the trash bag tucked under her arm and her knapsack—loaded with schoolbooks, masking tape, scissors, and gel for her hair—on her back. Before stuffing it in the bag, she'd noticed the uniform felt a little stiff from being new. Michelle smiled to herself. Give it a couple of weeks and some washing and her official practice uniform would be as comfortable as any of her old T-shirts. She just hoped it fit.

"Hi, sweetie!" Mrs. Dupree glanced up from reviewing invoices to greet Michelle. "How was your first day back?"

"Great, Mom." She dropped the bag on the counter. "Skye's in Teen Living with me. And guess what? So are Matt and a couple of the other guys. And our teacher, Miss Ashleigh, has this really cool Southern accent. She is so sharp. She bakes chocolate chip cookies, but she says it's perfectly fine because she knows how to burn off the calories teaching aerobics. It's too bad she wasn't here when Brian took Teen Living. He would have adored Miss Ashleigh," she said, imitating the teacher's drawl.

Her mother giggled. "I positively agree, Miss Scarlett. And what, pray tell, is this?" she asked, tapping the black bag.

Michelle reached inside and held the shirt up to her body. "Isn't it neat?" Taking her knapsack with her, Michelle grabbed her helmet and headed toward the bathroom to change. "It better not be too big," she hollered over her shoulder.

Carefully, Michelle hung her denim jumper on the back of the door. Then came the nicest surprise of the day: The uniform wasn't too big. In fact, considering it was supposed to be oversized, and she was already wearing Brian's hand-me-down shoulder pads, Number 4 fit perfectly. Now for the hard part.

Michelle stared at herself in the mirror and sighed. She'd never give herself as good a head wrap as Sandy had, but she was going to try. Reluctantly, she took the gel, masking tape, and scissors out of her knapsack and set them on the sink.

Taking a deep breath, she pumped a glob of gel in one hand. Then, closing her eyes, she began oozing the goo through each strand of hair. A raw egg couldn't have felt worse. Wrapping the elastic band around her hair and securing it in a ponytail was the easy part.

By the time Michelle was finished, it was a sure bet: Sandy had definitely done a better job. The tape held most of her hair down, but here and there, little greasy tufts poked through. Instead of looking like a mummy, she looked like someone with a scalp disease. Oh, well, Michelle thought as she placed her new Eagles blue-and-gold helmet on her head, if she ever gave up football, she could get a job doing a TV commercial. She could be a kid losing her hair in front of the bathroom mirror. All the bald people in the world would turn off their televisions and run to the drug store to buy Marvelous Miracle Hair Restorer. Maybe she would get an award for her performance and have to make a speech.

Michelle fastened the chin strap and put everything back in her knapsack.

"Oh, there you are, Number Four," her father said as she opened the bathroom door. He handed her a soft drink and a candy bar.

"Thanks, Dad." Michelle stared at both, not sure how she could eat or drink while wearing the helmet. She certainly couldn't take it off. Seeing their daughter's mummified head with tufts of hair sticking out would only make her parents ask all sorts of awkward questions.

"Um, I'm kind of in a hurry, Dad," she said finally. "You know, first practice and all. Coach Brown doesn't like kids showing up late. How about if I take it with me?"

"Fine, but give your old dad a kiss."

Michelle leaned forward and butted him lightly with the face guard. "Good enough?" She laughed.

Her father kissed his fingers and pressed them lightly on her helmet. "I guess that will have to do. Your mom and I will see you at home."

Michelle slung her cleats over her shoulder. Still wearing her helmet, and carrying her soft drink and candy bar, she hurried back toward school and her first practice for the Eagles football team.

"Mitch! Jocko! Over here." Michelle had barely come

through the gate and already the coach was shouting at her.

Michelle trotted across the field to where Coach Brown was studying his clipboard. A moment later she was joined by the biggest boy she'd ever seen. Jocko was a mountain. Understatement. He was the Swiss Alps. On a hot day, she'd want to stand in his shade.

"You want me, Coach?" The boy gazed anxiously at Coach Brown with small but eager blue eyes.

Coach Brown rested his hand on Jocko's broad shoulder. "I want you and Mitch at the far end practicing your punts and kicks. First thirty minutes, punts. Next thirty minutes, field goals from fifteen yards, twenty-five yards, and thirty yards. Then it's extra points until practice is over. You got that?"

"Yes, sir, but—"

"But what, Zimmerman?"

"I thought I was your kicker."

If Michelle didn't see the big body standing in front of her, she would have thought a little dink kid was asking that question. The way Jocko Joey was whining, she couldn't help but feel a little sorry for him.

"You are, Baby Cakes. But so is Mitch, and I told you to expect to play defense, too."

Jocko's shoulders slumped. Michelle could barely hear him mumble, "I don't want to play defense."

If Coach Brown heard, he ignored it. He turned to Michelle. "Mitch, that helmet fit you? Helmets are supposed to protect your head, not cover up your entire face. That one looks a little big."

Inside the helmet, Michelle gulped. "Feels fine, sir," she mumbled in her gravelly voice. If he asked her to take it off, she was dead meat.

He didn't. Instead he put his hands on both sides and tried giving the helmet a twist. When it didn't budge, he stepped back. "Fooled me," he said, looking surprised. "You have a bigger head than I thought."

Under the helmet where the coach couldn't see, Michelle rolled her eyes. Obviously, that was supposed to be a compliment. "Thank you, sir."

Coach Brown turned his attention back to Jocko. "Mitch is new here. I want you to show him the ropes." He nodded toward the far end of the field.

Jocko glanced at Michelle. His lip curled slightly. "Kind of a pipsqueak, isn't he, Coach?" he said.

Michelle pretended not to hear. Instead, she reached under the waistband of her uniform pants and scratched. Then, just to be safe, she aimed for a dandelion and spit, missing it entirely. It didn't matter.

"Well, maybe not." When Jocko spit, the dandelion almost fell off its stem.

A few minutes later, as she and Jocko dragged a duffel bag filled with footballs toward the goalposts, Michelle couldn't help smiling to herself. Big brother Brian had been right. She and Jocko weren't exactly spitting buddies, but it was a start.

It turned out that Jocko's name was Joey Zimmerman in the classroom but Jocko on the field. "So, Mitch, what grade are you in?" Jocko Joey squinted at her. "Sixth?"

First, he'd insulted her size. Now he was calling her a baby. Michelle fought to keep her voice steady and low. "Nope."

"Seventh."

"Yep."

"Seventh, huh?" Joey gave her a closer look. "So how come I've never seen you around?" he asked suspiciously. "You taking shop?"

"Nope."

"What about lunch?" Joey demanded, not letting up. "I never saw you in the cafeteria. You take last lunch?"

"Yep."

"Huh. I thought I looked everybody over real good in the lunchroom. Little as you are, I would have remembered you, don't you think?"

"Yep."

Jocko Joey set the ball on the ground. "Hey, is that all you can say? Yep and nope?"

She was sweating bullets and thinking about actually putting some gravel in her mouth, because keeping her voice unnaturally low was real hard. "Yep."

Jocko stopped to swat a pesky fly. "I can tell this is going to be a heck of a long practice," he grumbled. "You'd think if the coach could find us a backup kicker, he could have at least found someone who could talk."

It was almost a relief when Jocko switched subjects.

"Hey!" Jocko suddenly brightened. "Maybe that cute sevie is in some of your classes. Is she? A girl about as big as my little finger?"

He held up his finger in case Mitchell didn't understand. Michelle shrugged, not saying a word.

"She has a neat laugh," Joey went on. "I heard it in the cafeteria when I was in line for my third tray."

For a minute it was almost like Jocko had slipped into a trance. He stared off into space with the goofiest expression Michelle had ever seen on a boy. If she didn't know better, she would have said Jocko was in love.

"I thought I saw her in Teen Living, but there was a bunch of kids between me and her."

Suddenly, Joey slapped his beefy thigh with his hand. "No more girl stuff. I kick first. Here, hold the ball. Twirl it around so I don't see the laces."

Being careful to keep her head down, Michelle squatted on the ground and positioned the ball, using one finger to hold it at a slight angle.

"Why don't you want to see the laces?" She almost didn't ask for fear her voice would give her away, but she was too curious not to.

For a minute, Joey seemed surprised. "You don't know?" He stared at her. "Don't tell me this is the first time you ever played football."

Michelle pretended to be brushing blades of grass away from the football. "Yep."

"You're kidding." Joey raised his helmet above his ears and scratched his head. "You never played football before?"

"Nope."

"And now you think you might beat me out for the kicking position and force me to play defense?"

Michelle took a deep breath. She glanced at him out of the corner of her eye. "Yep."

Suddenly, Joey was holding on to his sides and laughing like Michelle had just said the funniest thing he'd ever heard.

Michelle scowled. What was the big joke?

Replacing his helmet, Joey smirked like he'd won the lottery. "Well, hey. If you never played football before, of course you wouldn't know about the laces." He paused to catch his breath. "I don't like looking at the laces before I kick. It's bad luck." He eyed Michelle curiously. "You're not superstitious, are you, Mitchell?"

"No way."

"Good. Then you won't care how the ball is placed. That makes holding it easier for me."

Remembering Brian's pregame superstitions regarding gaseous and smelly things to eat made Jocko's fears easy to believe. If Brian could load up on garlic, beans, and pizza for good luck, she guessed Joey could avoid looking at laces. She turned the ball around and waited.

"Aw, shucks. That ball must be going flat," Joey said when his last kick went wide and to the left. "It's your turn. Why don't you do both of us a favor? Try kicking yours in the same spot so we don't have to walk all over the place fetching balls."

It was Michelle's turn to smirk. "Sorry, Jocko," she said cockily. "Mine go through the uprights."

"We'll just see about that," Joey retorted. He yanked on his face guard and spat before carefully positioning Michelle's first ball with the laces showing.

For some peculiar reason, not all of Michelle's kicks were as accurate as before. First day jitters, she told herself as they trudged downfield for longer yardage. Her field goal kicks were equally inconsistent, a real puzzle.

Another nuisance was Joey's boring conversation about his wannabe sevie girlfriend. Finally, after two hours on the field, they returned to the fifteen yard line to practice their extra point kicks. Michelle had already kicked hers. It was Joey's turn.

"Aw, man." Joey wiped his hands on his shirt while waiting for Michelle to position the ball. "Did I tell you that little sevie is sure a looker? Mmmmm-mm."

"Only a thousand fifty times, Joey," Michelle muttered under her breath.

"A looker like that probably already has a boyfriend," Joey dragged on. "Maybe. Maybe not. If she does, I could just . . ."

Bored beyond reason, Michelle held the ball in place. A big silver plane was cruising under a line of level clouds. If it increased its altitude by half an inch, it would disappear from sight. If only the same thing would happen to Joey.

Joey barreled toward the ball. But with his mind focused on the sevie of his dreams, his foot wasn't aimed for the ball. Instead the force of all of his one hundred and sixty pounds was directed at Michelle's hand.

"Yeeee-ow!" Michelle grabbed her hand and brought it to her chest. Then she rolled over, doubled up in pain.

CHAPTER 8

"**I**t's not broken, but it sure hurts," Michelle told Sandy on the phone. "Matt's already called twice and he's calling again after dinner. He's probably worried about my future in sports. He told me to use a bag of frozen peas as a compress, and you know what? It works. Maybe he should be a doctor or something."

"Or something," Sandy said in a sing-songy voice. "Maybe he's working up the nerve to ask you to the dance. Remember the one after the game? Everyone's going. I'm in charge of streamers. Oh, my gosh," she suddenly exclaimed. "How are you going to prepare for school tomorrow? You won't be able to do your hair. Do you want me to come over and help?"

Michelle winced as she adjusted the bag of peas. The school dance was definitely not high on her list of priorities.

"Thanks," she said. "I'll manage. But I do need help keeping my injury a secret—especially from Jocko Joey. If he sees me as Michelle with a sore hand, it'll blow my cover. I can't even put an Ace bandage on it."

"Honestly," Sandy said. "That Joey is the biggest pain. Every time I turn around, he's practically in my face."

"Hey," Michelle said. "You must be the one he has a crush on. It's all he talks about at practice. That's why he kicked my hand. I tell you, he was in la-la-land."

"Hmmm." Sandy paused. "Maybe that's why he's always following me around when I'm conducting my interviews. But I try to avoid him. He's so obvious. Anyway, you're right—we can't let anybody find out about your hand. Which hand is it?"

"Right," Michelle answered. "And I'm right-handed."

"Oooh," Sandy groaned. "Double major catastrophe."

Michelle didn't need to be reminded. Not then nor the next morning when she had to haul all her football stuff back downstairs, through the kitchen, and out to the garage without so much as a whimper, because if her mom found out about her hand, there would be all sorts of questions that Michelle would not want to answer. Later, after struggling with her knapsack, she had to settle for carrying it into school on her right shoulder. When pain shot down her arm like a streak of lightning, she gritted her teeth and kept walking toward homeroom. Letting Sandy carry her knapsack or dragging it by her left hand would have been lots easier. More obvious, too.

Luckily, in math, the seventh grade took standardized achievement tests, so all Michelle had to do was circle A, B, C, or D. In English, her teacher began reading the novel they would dissect the next week. Social studies was spent watching a filmstrip.

By the time Michelle waltzed into Teen Living, she was wondering how long her good fortune would last. Miss Ashleigh must have read her mind, because she assigned her and Matt to the same table to learn how to bake brownies from a cookbook instead of a box.

The smell of chocolate brownies baking in the oven had everyone drooling. While Matt thoughtfully held the timer, Michelle turned the dial with her left hand. When the timer went off, he grabbed the potholders. "I got it," he called, opening the oven. When he set the brownies on the table, his face was flushed from the heat.

In the back of her mind, Michelle could hear Sandy gush, "Now when the two of you get married, you won't be stuck in the kitchen. Matt will have great cooking skills."

Looking at the cute freckles parading across Matt's nose, Michelle felt her face turn hot—and she wasn't anywhere near the oven.

In the cafeteria, Michelle was trying to balance her tray with her left hand and right forearm when Skye bumped into her. Michelle winced. For a moment, she thought she might keel over from the pain.

"What's the matter?" Skye grabbed Michelle's tray. "You look like you might faint."

Instinctively, Michelle brought her right hand protectively close to her chest. "I hurt my hand at practice," she admitted.

"Oh, my gosh! I knew you'd get hurt!" Skye shrieked.

"Shhh! I don't want anyone to know."

They sat down quickly at the table where Sandy was saving two places.

"I told you football was too dangerous," Skye told Sandy. "She's only had one day of practice and already she's practically debilitated. This is Wednesday," she said, turning to Michelle. "You have to get through practice today and Thursday, and be ready to play on Friday. You'll only make that injury worse. I don't like this at all. You could become permanently damaged."

Michelle fumbled with her milk carton. Finally, Sandy grabbed it and opened it under the table.

"Skye, you're overreacting," Michelle said.

"I am not. If you get really, really hurt and can't play basketball, I'm never going to speak to you again." Skye sniffed. "You need to keep that hand elevated."

Michelle winked at Sandy. "Thanks. I'll talk to Coach Brown. Maybe he'll tape it to my helmet."

Sandy giggled.

Skye pushed her chair back and stood up, cheeks flaming. "You guys can laugh all you want, but it's not funny." She jabbed Sandy on the shoulder. "You better go to both practices and make sure she protects her hand. Because if you don't, I will."

Sandy rolled her eyes and shook her head impatiently. "I will, I will." She waited until Skye was out of earshot. "Honestly, I've never heard Skye sound so assertive. She's really upset."

"I know." Michelle sighed. "She's not the only one." When she was sure no one was looking, she tried picking up an apple with her left hand. That was when she knocked the open milk carton onto the floor.

In just two days, Michelle, Matt, Rani, and Lamar had their morning and after-practice routines in place. As long as Michelle didn't change in the locker room after practice and rode home with one of them, no one was likely to discover her true identity. All she had to do was keep her helmet on and her head down.

"You're not to worry about the helmet or be confused," Rani told his grandfather, who picked them up from practice on Wednesday. "Our man Mitch has a growing need to be helmeted at all times."

"I still feel rotten about Mitch's hand," Joey told Matt halfway through Thursday's practice.

"Yeah?" Matt sounded sore. "Then maybe you could make it up to him by doing all the holding. It's a sure bet he won't be able to hold for you, unless you plan on kicking his other hand out of commission."

Joey stepped up to Matt and grabbed him by the T-shirt. "Are you saying I did it on purpose?"

"I'm saying it was pretty darn convenient." Matt sucked in his gut and puffed out his chest. "Everyone knows how badly you want to be first-string kicker."

Fortunately, Coach Brown wandered over before their words turned into a fight. "Okay, men!" he shouted. He blew his whistle loud and long. "Kicking squad, hustle front and center. Joey, let's run page thirty-five in the playbook, the clutch play. Mitch, watch and learn. We may need this play at some crucial point."

Joey's eyebrows furrowed. He raised his finger to ask Coach a question, then thought better of it.

Standing next to Matt, Michelle recognized the play Coach had just called. Probably Jocko hadn't done any more than look at the pictures.

The kicking squad assumed their positions and waited patiently for Joey to stop prancing in place. Impatient, Lamar yelled, "Are you ready for some football?" Joey stopped prancing and the front line dissolved in laughter. Finally, Neil hiked the ball to Joey.

"SHOOT!" Joey yelled at the top of his lungs.

Except for their helmets turning as they looked at each other in complete bewilderment, the guys didn't move a muscle.

"SHOOT!" Jocko yelled again. "SHOOT! SHOOT! BANG! BANG!"

"Hey, Coach," Neil shouted. "Does he mean fire?"

Coach was holding his head in frustration as he paced the sidelines. He threw the clipboard down on the ground. "Of all the . . . yes!"

"Fire!" Neil yelled. "Fire! Fire! Fire!"

"Yeah. Run, you guys!" Jocko barked after them.

Neil and two hefty blockers held the line as the rest of the guys tore down the field. In a frenzied panic, Joey heaved the ball to no one in particular.

"No! No! NO!!!" Coach exploded. "There wasn't anyone within miles of that bomb. You want a penalty for intentional grounding? Get with it, Jocko!" He was writing furiously on his clipboard.

When he looked up, he stared keenly in Michelle's direction.

Uh-oh.

Not wanting the coach to scrutinize her too closely, Michelle picked up a football and started toward the far side of the field where she and Joey had practiced the day before. A few minutes later, Joey was trotting beside her.

"Who invented that dumb play? That's what I want to know," Joey grumbled. "Besides, 'shoot' is a better word than 'fire.' Any dope knows that."

Michelle had her own problems to think about. Her injured hand shouldn't have affected her kicking foot, but absolutely none of her kicks today or yesterday had been any good. If she didn't know better, she would have thought she'd never put her foot to a pigskin in her whole life.

Strangely enough, both days Joey had been grinning the way Hercules did while he got his tummy rubbed.

"Well, I wouldn't worry," he said as he placed his bear paw on Michelle's shoulder. "Unless you think you might choke during Friday's game against the Warhawks. You know, your first game with everyone in the stands watching you kick the ball. Just you, only you, having to make the crucial field goal." Joey threw back his head and laughed. "You've got to get better. Heck, you can't get much worse." He turned and spit out of the side of his mouth.

Michelle couldn't resist the challenge. Keeping her head at the right angle, her toes and elbows out, she gathered her saliva, rolling it around on her tongue before letting it go in one long, weed-killing spit.

When she looked up, Matt was walking toward them.

Whoops! Michelle grimaced. She'd better remember not to scratch. But apparently, Matt hadn't walked all the way across the field to see her. Instead, he extended his hand to Joey.

"Hey, man, sorry about that scene," he apologized. "Guess I'm keyed up about playing the Warhawks."

Joey kicked at a piece of loose turf. "No sweat. Hey, you're smart." He dug deep into his pocket. "What do you think this means?" he asked, pulling out a folded slip of paper and handing it to Matt.

Matt frowned as he unfolded the note. "Where did you find this?"

"In my locker."

"Mitch, do you know anything about this?" Matt showed the note to Michelle.

!!! WARNING !!!
Someone let MORE girls in the boys' locker room!

Michelle froze.

Meanwhile, Joey, his helmet cradled in his arm and his eyes narrowed into slits, slowly surveyed the playing field. Finally, his eyes rested on Michelle. "Have you seen any girls in our locker room?"

She shook her head, but Joey wasn't paying attention.

"I didn't smell any perfume," he went on. "The toilets were still up. Oh, gross!" he exploded. "I left my underwear on the floor in front of my locker. Maybe we better tell Coach," he added. "This could be serious."

"Nah," Matt said, as if he thought the whole thing was silly. "That's crazy. It's bad enough now with Coach calling Lamar a powder puff and offering to buy Rani a pink tutu. Besides, it's only someone playing a joke. How could girls be in our locker room?"

"Yeah, I guess you're right," Joey said. "With all of us guys, somebody would have seen them. There's no place to hide in the locker room." He studied the note again before wadding it up and sticking it in his mouth to chew.

Michelle tried shrugging it off. "Cool it, Jocko."

"Yeah," Matt agreed. "It's nothing. Probably someone saw us practicing and thinks we play like girls."

Behind Joey's back, "Mitchell" rolled his eyes at Matt and made a face.

"Hey, man, that better be all it is." Joey replaced his

helmet and snapped his chin strap. "There are some places girls just don't belong." He spiked the football for emphasis. "Right, Mitch?"

Michelle gulped. "Right," she agreed, almost forgetting to use her deep voice.

Suddenly, Joey turned, and holding the ball in front of him, gave it a hard kick.

"Good punt," Matt said appreciatively. But Joey didn't hear. He'd already charged after the football, bellowing like an angry bull.

"I'm glad he's gone," Matt said as soon as Joey left. "Coach Brown wants to know what's the matter with your head?"

Michelle frowned. "There's nothing wrong with my head."

"He means the way you keep it down all the time. He's complaining because he can't see your face."

Michelle and Matt burst out laughing, a welcome relief after having seen Joey's note.

"I told him you were really shy," Matt said. "I mean, *really* shy."

Michelle nodded. "Good thinking."

Matt gave her a crooked smile. He was nervously tossing a football back and forth between his hands. "Um . . . I was wondering . . . um . . . are you going to that school dance in the cafeteria? Because if you are, I'll probably see you there."

Michelle gulped. Afterward, she would try to remember what she'd told him. Sandy would want to know.

CHAPTER 9

The red-and-white banner was the first thing Michelle saw when she entered school Friday morning. It was hanging from the ceiling in Jefferson's front hall, anchored by featherless rubber chickens tied by their legs, heads dangling in defeat. PLUCK THE WARHAWKS, the banner said. Another banner, this one bright blue and gold, proclaimed GO EAGLES from its spot over the salad bar in the cafeteria. The Pep Squad had spent days creating the colorful streamers and plastering the school walls with posters.

Instead of last period, there was a pep rally. When the cheerleaders cartwheeled across the stage in a whirl of blue and gold, everyone stood up and cheered. Like perky ponies, the girls pranced into position, waving their festive pom-poms.

"Give me a T! Give me an E!" they shouted into their megaphones. Everyone in the gym joined in, including Michelle. When they finished spelling the word *TEAM,* Coach Brown dashed up the center aisle, followed by the Eagles football squad. Again, everyone stood up, including Michelle. This time, their cheers raised the rafters.

"Coach wanted to know why Mitch wasn't at the pep rally," Matt told Michelle afterward. "I don't like to lie, but this time it was necessary." He shrugged helplessly. "I told him that Mitch was being fitted for braces and couldn't get out of his orthodontist appointment."

Michelle rubbed her tongue across her teeth. She didn't need braces. But now, thanks to Matt, Coach Brown was going to think she had a mouth like a jigsaw puzzle. Oh well, it was just another excuse to keep her head down and her lips zipped tight.

"Remember Coach's schedule," Matt reminded her. "Everyone in the locker room, dressed and ready for the final game plan at six-thirty. Be at the door and I'll let you in."

Michelle took a deep breath and shuddered. "I don't know if I can go through with this."

"Coach Brown is depending on you," Matt said, putting his hand on Michelle's shoulder.

"I don't know why. My kicks aren't all that good."

"They were during tryouts. That's what Coach remembers. We're all hoping that you turn out to be a clutch-type player. Some people thrive on pressure."

Just then, Michelle spied Joey lumbering around the corner. "Uh-oh, time for Michelle to disappear." She couldn't chance Joey seeing her up close and recognizing her as Mitch. There was no way to predict what his reaction would be.

Michelle took the school bus home, a long ride without Sandy, who had stayed to help decorate for the dance. It was all Sandy could talk about. Honestly, you would have thought Matt had invited Michelle to Disney World, or Hawaii—or anyplace more exotic than the gym.

"He didn't exactly invite me," Michelle had told Sandy the night before when she'd left her dress, pumps, and overnight bag at Sandy's house. "All he said was that he would see me there."

"Same thing," Sandy insisted fiercely. "Anyway, my dad agreed to drive. By the time we change and get beautified and pick up Skye, we'll be fashionably late for the dance. Don't you love it? Matt will be panting in joyful anticipation."

As Michelle stepped off the school bus, she was trying to picture Matt at the dance. She floated into the kitchen—and stopped abruptly. Brian was standing at the counter brandishing a hammer and chisel.

"What in the world are you doing?" Michelle asked, letting her knapsack slide to the floor.

"What does it look like? I'm fixing chili."

Apparently, their mother had taken chili out of the freezer and left it in a plastic bowl to thaw. It hadn't.

"It's too big for the pot," Brian said. He'd already broken off little bits and pieces. Hercules eagerly lapped up whatever flew to the floor.

"I hate to burst your bubble, Brian, but all you have to do is throw the bowl in the microwave."

Brian set the hammer and chisel down with a clunk. "I knew that," he mumbled, sticking the bowl in the microwave.

Michelle punched in the numbers as Brian began rooting around in the spice drawer. "Mom never makes it right." He set little containers of chili powder, garlic powder, and onion salt on the counter.

Michelle waited until the timer dinged before handing Brian the oven mitts. "Smells good," she said as Brian poked at the chili with a wooden spoon.

Brian took a whiff. "Not quite." He dumped in more ingredients. "You want some?" he said a few minutes later, holding the bowl out to her.

Michelle's eyes started to water. Quickly, she stepped out of range. So did Hercules. Under normal circumstances, he would have hung around the kitchen expecting handouts. But even Hercules knew better than to touch that chili-flavored time bomb.

"No way."

"You'll be sorry," Brian cautioned. "Take it from me, chili is great for defense. All I have to do is breathe on the opposition and they topple right over. Come to think of it, if you show up for tonight's game smelling like mouthwash, they're liable to think something's fishy."

"Maybe I could just rub some chili on my skin."

"What? And not eat any? You don't know what you're missing! Speaking of which," Brian said, swallowing a humongous load of pinto beans, "you're lucky Mom and Dad have that big bank reception tonight and can't go to the game. You know Dad. He would have walked up to Coach Brown, slapped him on the back, and said a hearty 'So how's my girl doing? Keeping the rest of the guys on their toes, is she? Yuk, yuk, yuk.'"

Michelle grabbed an apple out of a bowl. "I wouldn't mind them seeing me," she said between bites. "They came to all of my basketball games."

Brian was leaning over the bowl of chili and really shoveling it in. Michelle could hardly stand to watch, it looked so gross.

"So how are you planning on handling the locker-room logistics?" he asked through a bulging mouthful.

"The same as practice. It's not a big deal," Michelle said, blowing off her earlier doubts. "I'm getting a ride over with Lamar, and I'll already be dressed for the game. I have to lie low for a half hour, and then Matt's meeting me at the locker-room door. They're taking care of me at halftime, too. It's like you said, Brian. Nobody recognizes me with my shoulder pads and helmet on."

"Sounds good." Brian raised his eyebrows and grinned. "You got potty break figured out?"

"Yep. I won't even be *near* the boys' toilets."

"What about the after-game showers?"

"What about them?"

"It's not like home. There's no shower curtain. Five seconds into the locker room and the whole team is buck naked."

Michelle stared at Brian. "No way! I only have five seconds?" she squeaked in panic. "I can't do that!"

Stunned, she picked up the phone and dialed Matt's number. Behind her, Brian laughed loudly through his chili.

Michelle gulped. Matt wasn't home. Lamar was the only one she'd see before the game, and there was no way she would ask Lamar about nakedness. Asking Matt would be bad enough.

Matt opened the locker room door. His face was flushed. "Quick, get in here. Coach is about to start."

"Wait a second, Matt. We've got to talk," Michelle said urgently. "What about the naked showers?"

Matt's eyes flew open. "Huh?"

86

"Dupree! Peterson!" Coach hollered. "Get over here."

Judging by the startled expression on Matt's face, he hadn't thought about the naked showers either.

"Mitch, I've got you down doing all the kicking. You can handle it," Coach said, reading from his clipboard. "Matt, quarterback. Joey, you're in as left tackle."

Anyone else would have been happy. Not Jocko Joey.

"Aw, please, Coach," Jocko begged. "I want to kick."

"Joey, quit whining and do your job. Two-position guys have to be flexible. Mitch, be ready for kickoff."

Angry, Jocko pushed in front of Michelle, shoving her with his elbows. At the same time, she got a horrific whiff of onions. She'd have to remember to stay upwind.

"Okay, guys! Do it!" Coach was clapping his hands and shouting. "Go! Go! Win! Win!"

Yelling and waving their helmets in the air, the Eagles ran onto the athletic field, where their screams were joined by cheerleaders and fans. So what if Number 4 was the only one wearing a helmet instead of waving it? If it looked weird and itched like crazy, Michelle as Mitch didn't have a choice.

Standing by herself, Michelle watched as Matt and two other players walked to the center of the field to join the referees and a couple of Warhawks for the coin toss. A few minutes later the announcement rang through the loudspeakers.

"Ladies and gentlemen! The Warhawks have won the toss and have elected to receive."

Before Michelle knew it, she was on the field with the rest of the squad. She kicked the ball deep to the Warhawks, putting the Eagles in good position. Even so, at the end of the second quarter, the score was 7–0 in the

Warhawks' favor. Matt hadn't even brought the team close enough for Michelle to attempt a field goal.

Michelle leaned against a portable net set up near the sidelines and watched the game clock. She waited until the clock reached the two-minute mark before casually wandering toward the end of the bench.

As soon as the whistle blew, Matt, Lamar, and Rani ran toward her. Smoothly, Michelle slipped along beside them as they loped toward the locker room. Once inside, she found an empty bench in the very back of the locker room and sat down. A few minutes later, Rani and Matt plopped down beside her.

"Not to fear. We'll shield you from all sides," Rani whispered while Matt dropped a white towel on her knees.

The guys had removed their helmets and had towels draped over their heads or around their sweaty necks. Quickly, Michelle ducked her helmeted head behind Lamar, who was casually standing in front of her. She hung the towel over her helmet like a ghost on Halloween.

"Don't do that," Matt whispered. "That's too obvious." When he pushed the towel off her helmet, his fingers lightly touched her neck, giving her the shivers.

Coach stormed into the locker room for his halftime pep talk. "I want you guys to listen up," he barked. "Can you hear me?"

"Yes, sir," they all shouted at once.

"Who's that with his helmet on? Mitchell!"

Michelle jumped a mile. "Yes, sir!"

Coach rolled his eyes and looked up at the ceiling. He shook his head and began to pace. "The Warhawks are a good team, but we're better. You got that?"

"Yes, sir."

"Mitchell?"

"Yes, sir!"

The demanding tone of Coach Brown's voice never let up as he revved the team. Finally he screamed, "Okay, men. Let's get out there and fight! WIN!"

The Eagles surged off the benches—all except for Michelle, who held back as Coach Brown and the pepped-up Eagles stampeded out of the locker room.

Then there was only deathly silence. A half minute later, Matt was back.

"Whew! I told the coach I forgot something." Matt grabbed his helmet while nodding his head toward the toilets. "Do you need those?"

Suddenly, they heard a loud crash behind them. Michelle whirled in time to see Joey coming out of one of the stalls. No way was she going to the bathroom now.

"What are you doing in here, Jocko?" Matt asked, obviously angry that he'd almost blown Michelle's cover.

"Double checking." Jocko peered around the trash can. "You didn't see any girls in here, did you, Helmet Head?" He slapped her on the side of the helmet.

Jocko turned to Matt. "Hey! That's what we'll call him, Helmet Head. Mitchell's too long a name for this mouse."

Nobody went anywhere in the third quarter. The Eagles couldn't score, but thanks to Michelle's lofty punts and the Eagles' courageous defense, neither could the Warhawks. Finally, in the fourth quarter, the Warhawks broke loose with a devastatingly long pass. They were flying in for sure! And then, when all hope seemed lost,

Jocko sacked the quarterback on the fifteen yard line, forcing a fumble.

The bleachers rocked!

"Joe-ey! Jo-ey! Jo-ey!"

The Warhawks left the field in a daze while Matt and the Eagles' offense rolled in. Momentum was everything! Matt ran a screen play and an end-around. He tried a flea-flicker, and when that didn't work, he carried the ball himself for another first down. Michelle was so proud.

Rani took the ball in for the touchdown.

The electronic scoreboard was blinking: Eagles 6, Warhawks 7.

Gulp! Michelle felt every eye in the stadium focused on her. It was up to her to tie the game.

Jocko rapped his knuckles on Michelle's helmet. She almost jumped out of her skin. "You ready, Helmet Head?" he barked so loud everyone could hear.

"Yo, Helmet Head!" Neil hollered as he and the rest of the kicking squad waited for Number 4 to kick the tying point.

Michelle stared at the ground as she started across the field. In her mind, she rehearsed her technique. She pictured herself making contact with the ball, felt it leaving her toe, flying straight and true.

Neil snapped the ball to Jocko, who set it in place. With her heart banging in her chest, Michelle made her approach.

Almost as soon as the ball soared between the uprights, the whistle blew. The game was over. Eagles 7, Warhawks 7. The fans went wild, screaming and yelling and thumping their feet on the bleachers.

The rest of the guys had their helmets under their arms as they started toward the middle of the field to congratulate each other for a good game. Not Michelle. Helmet on, head down, she shook a few hands before slipping back toward the Eagles' bench. She was thinking about what Brian had said about the showers. Somehow she needed to escape before Coach Brown waved everyone into the locker room. If he didn't see her, he might not miss her.

"Good game, Helmet Head," a couple of the guys remarked.

"Teamwork," Michelle muttered, careful to keep her voice low as she continued walking past the bleachers.

"Yeah," Jocko grumbled. "But just remember you wouldn't have made that big point if I hadn't forced that fumble on the Warhawks' fifteen."

"Yeah," Michelle said in her gravelliest voice. "Great play, Jocko." She resisted the urge to spit.

She didn't have to. Jocko's was thick and powerful enough for both of them. "Uh, will you be at the dance?" he asked, wiping the leftover spit from his mouth with the back of his hand. "I might need your help finding that cute sevie I've been telling you about."

Michelle scratched her neck. "Nah. Don't think so." She waited until they were almost to the school building before dropping to the ground as though to tie her shoelaces. Crowds of parents and kids were leaving through the side gate. As soon as the guys were out of sight, she slipped through the gate along with everyone else. Sandy found her right away.

"Fantastic game, Michelle!" Sandy exclaimed as they hurried toward the car. "Your kick is going to make the perfect ending for my article. You couldn't have done me a better favor. You should have seen Skye sitting with Miss Ashleigh. They absolutely went bonkers."

Michelle, helmet on and still disguised as Mitch, whirled around. "Shhh! Don't use my name. Somebody's going to hear you."

Even in the shadows, Michelle could see the hurt expression on Sandy's face. She felt instantly sorry. "Do you want to know why I didn't go in the locker room after the game? You won't believe what Brian told me!" she said, leaning toward her best friend.

"Details, pul-ease!" Sandy whipped her notebook out of her purse. "What I really need is a tape recorder."

"Except you can't use it. This is strictly off the record."

"Privileged information? Secret stuff? Come on, blab! Quick!"

Michelle sighed. "Not now. Not here. Later. Soon!"

"Wait till you see the gym. It is so cool. This is going to be the best dance ever." Sandy smoothed her dress closer to her legs as Skye climbed into the backseat to sit with her and Michelle.

"I hope so," Michelle said. "Aren't you the least bit concerned about Jocko?"

"Sandy and Jocko?" Skye said, bewildered.

Sandy rolled her eyes. She shook her head and blew air out of her mouth in a little puff. "Sorry to disappoint, but I've made so many conquests this past week that I am completely unavailable."

Skye started to choke. "Maybe if I stand close enough, you could give me some of your leftovers— jerky Jocko not included."

Michelle was glad that no one ever called Matt a jerk. The more she thought about it, Matt was a lot like Hercules: loyal and dependable. She wondered where she should look for him at the dance. Would he really—as Sandy had said—be waiting for her with joyful anticipation?

Matt was watching for her at the refreshment table.

"Hey, Michelle. You got here just in time. The good cookies are almost gone. Here, I saved you one." He handed her a gigantic chocolate chip cookie on a yellow paper plate. "Do you want some punch?"

She was surprised by how good the cup of cold punch felt against her hand.

"Does it still hurt?" Matt said, noticing her look.

"Not too much," she answered as they moved toward the middle of the gym. The music was loud and had a good beat.

"That's a neat song. Do you want to dance?" he asked after a while.

He squashed their paper cups and plates and tossed them into the trash can. Then he took her hand. She winced. It wasn't a big wince, but Matt still noticed.

"Sorry," he said. "Other hand."

Laughing and blushing, Matt hurried around to her other side and took her left hand to lead her out onto the floor.

They danced to three fast songs, but who was counting? Then they danced to a slow song. That was harder. No matter how they tried, their feet kept bumping into each other, a problem they never had on the basketball court. And holding her right arm up so that her right hand barely touched Matt's palm without getting painfully squeezed was a challenge only the Statue of Liberty would understand.

Bright blue-and-gold balloons bobbed from the ceiling as they swayed in time to the beat. Suddenly, Joey's round pumpkin face loomed over Matt's shoulder with a grin as wide and happy as a jack-o'-lantern. Michelle noticed something else. He was staring directly at her. Worse, he was wearing the same dazed la-la-land expression as he had when he'd blabbered on and on about his mysterious little sevie.

Oh, my gosh! Michelle's hurt hand covered her mouth in shock. *She* was Joey's sevie!

CHAPTER 16

Sandy called an emergency meeting in the park the next day.

"What a total catastrophe! Something has to be done fast!" she exclaimed to everyone involved in Michelle's dilemma.

Matt threw Michelle a questioning glance, which Michelle answered with a shrug. "What are you talking about?" he asked.

Sandy threw her arms wide over her head. "Only the most crucial, most devastating development involving Michelle and Jocko. That's what!"

Oh, embarrassment city.

"Apparently," Sandy continued, "jerky Jocko Joey has a huge unwelcome crush on Michelle."

Matt was staring at Sandy like she'd left all her marbles at the dance.

"So what?" Lamar said.

Sandy blinked her eyes at Lamar's unthinkable ignorance. "The problem is that if Jocko gets in Michelle's face too often, he'll discover that she's Mitch."

"Which would make her dead," Skye interjected.

Lamar nodded solemnly. "Coach would kick her off the team for sure."

Rani folded his arms across his chest. "And suspend all of us. This has always been a possibility."

Matt's face paled. "What do you want us to do?"

"I think it's perfectly obvious," Sandy said. "You simply have to tell Jocko that you're going with Michelle."

"What!" Michelle was shocked.

"Yes," Sandy replied, completely oblivious to Michelle's reaction. "That way Jocko will back off and leave her alone. It's the only way."

Maybe so, but Matt was turning red just thinking about it. He'd already pulled the neck of his T-shirt so badly out of shape he'd probably never be able to wear it again.

"Um, I guess I could do that," he said slowly. "What do you think, Michelle?"

Michelle felt her face flush as red as Matt's. As nice as it might turn out, being Matt's official girlfriend wasn't something she'd bargained for when she'd agreed to join the team—especially under these forced circumstances. "Um . . . as long as my parents don't find out. No offense, Matt, but they'd ground me for the rest of my life."

Matt nodded. "Mine, too. They want me going to college after high school, not getting married."

Lamar and Rani snickered.

"Oh, please," Skye said, disgusted.

"Here's what we do for starters." Sandy drew everyone near.

Talk about organization! On Monday, Sandy cornered

Joey after sewing class, begging a fake interview for the paper. Meanwhile, in the cafeteria, Lamar sent a group of sixth graders scrambling back in line for free French fries. It was a wild goose chase, of course, but it did net Michelle, Matt, and their friends a vacant table. Quickly, they swarmed to fill all the seats. When Jocko walked past searching for a place to sit after loading his third tray, Sandy positively beamed. "See. I told you this would work!"

"Quite. However, the cafeteria is not a problem," Rani interjected. "Joey focuses on food, not women, at lunchtime."

After sweating through school hours as Michelle, returning to the practice field that afternoon suited up and disguised as Mitch was a welcome relief. That is, until Jocko abandoned his defensive maneuvers and stomped out to midfield where Matt, Michelle, and the rest of the offense were working on field goal drills.

"Hey, Helmet Head," Jocko grunted loudly, obviously for Matt's benefit. "Too bad you missed the dance. Man, what lousy luck. I find the perfect girl and what do you know? She's dancing with the quarterback." He spit a sunflower seed dangerously close to where Matt was holding a football in position. Not getting the reaction he sorely wanted, Jocko pawed the turf like an angry bull. He spit another seed, still closer.

"Man," he groaned. "You should have seen Peterson here with his paws all over my sevie. It would have torn your heart out."

No fooling. Underneath her helmet, Michelle was dying a thousand deaths. So would Joey, if Matt had anything to say about it.

Michelle watched as Matt slowly rose from his crouched position next to the kicking tee. Behind him, the ball wobbled off the tee before rolling to the ground—just like Joey's head would in another second. Matt approached Joey, fists clenched, eyes like steel, jaw muscles working overtime.

"So, what's the deal? You going with her?" Jocko demanded. "What did you give her the other night—a ring?"

The way he said it was crude. So was the wink he threw Mitch. Michelle cringed. She didn't want any part of this guy thing.

"What's it to you?" Matt snarled.

"Everything!" Joey bellowed loud enough for the whole team to hear, including Coach Brown.

When Jocko spit the third seed, hitting Matt on the shoulder, Coach Brown exploded. "Jocko! Get over here now! Hit the dummies. Hard!" he shouted.

Michelle would have liked to hit a dummy, too—and she didn't mean a regulation tackling dummy either. But girls weren't supposed to hit or fight. It wasn't feminine. Funny, Michelle sniffed. Girls weren't supposed to play football either. Whoever made up the rules had gotten them all wrong.

The rest of the week was like baby-sitting a time bomb. Michelle's friends kept her isolated from Joey as best they could. Still, as the Eagles prepared for their second game, against the Atoms, no one knew exactly when Joey might explode.

On Friday, Michelle, Matt, Rani, and Lamar kept to their routine. She came to the game suited up and ready. By the time Matt opened the locker room door, Coach was already into his pep talk. He had a few last-minute X's and O's drawn on his chalkboard. Inside her helmet, Michelle smiled, thinking of Sandy's hugs and kisses.

By the end of the second quarter, the score was tied, 0–0. As before, at halftime Michelle scooted between Matt and Rani on a bench in the locker room with Lamar standing directly in front of her.

The rest of the guys came crashing in, followed by a roaring Coach Brown.

"Nothing to nothing!" he shouted. "What are you guys waiting for?"

Thwap! Something hard smacked an equipment bag.

Michelle tried not to tremble as locker doors slammed and Coach Brown's voice grew louder. Another *thwap!*, this time on the floor beside where they were sitting. Coach Brown had heaved a football.

"Double zero," he screamed louder still. He was cutting a path in their direction.

Double gulp!

"Not to worry, Michelle," Rani whispered. "This is but a harmless creature. Observe."

"I expect fast, hard action!" Coach's voice pierced her eardrums. "Okay, men. Let's go out there and defuse those Atoms! No more zeros on the board. Let's win!"

With a mighty cheer, Michelle and the boys tore out of the locker room.

The Atoms and Eagles were well matched. The Eagles defense didn't give any ground to the Atoms, but no matter what Matt and the Eagles offense tried, the score remained 0–0.

By the beginning of the fourth quarter, both teams were tired. Michelle, who had seen minimal action on the field, knew from experience that she had to stay focused. She tried mind drills, counting down from one hundred by threes. She ordered herself to concentrate. Anything to stay alert. Mistakes always came easier at the end of a game.

Suddenly, it was third down on the Atoms' twenty and long yardage.

"Mitch, you're on," Coach boomed. "Get out there and break that tie. It's up to you."

Seconds later, Neil hiked the ball to Jocko, who placed it precisely on the tee. Michelle's foot caught the ball square on the laces, sending it airborne but not far or high enough. Blocked kick!

Colors blurred before Michelle's eyes as both teams scrambled for the loose ball. An Atom had it!

Neat as a pin, he'd tucked the ball under his arm and started pumping toward Eagles' territory. But where were the Eagles? Most of them were frantically looking around to see who had the ball. They'd been caught completely off guard.

What else could Michelle do? There was only one person who could deny the Atoms their score. It was up to her.

In an instant, Michelle's adrenaline kicked into overdrive. With no time to think, she zoomed toward the Atom player until—*whomp!* She hit a brick wall and was out like a light.

When she came to, faces swarmed above her. Voices echoed. And that was only the beginning of her worst nightmare.

She'd lost her helmet.

The whole world, including Coach Brown, was peering down at a girl grotesquely disguised as a guy with masking-taped hair. Michelle closed her eyes tight. Maybe when she woke up, this would all be a dream. Sadly, it wasn't.

The way she knew this was real was because they were asking her the stupidest questions and she was giving the stupidest answers. How many fingers am I holding up, and what is your grandmother's last name? Suddenly, her mom and dad were bending over her and looking more concerned than ever.

"What happened?" she asked groggily. "Did I stop him? They didn't score, did they?"

"No," someone answered. "You forced a crucial fumble. You'll probably get MVP for that play."

Fat chance. Judging by the scowl on Coach Brown's face, her chances were slim to none.

She heard an ambulance wail.

"Hey, I don't need an ambulance," she pleaded. "I'm only a little winded. Hand me my helmet. At least let me walk off the field."

Her mother's hand pushed her back down. "Lie still, sweetie. Your helmet is right here beside you."

The medics hurried over with a stretcher.

"Cripes! Look at that!" Joey's obnoxious voice rang out above the crowd. "Hey, you guys. Helmet Head's a Conehead. And he's a she! And she's a girl!"

As they carried her off the field, Michelle could see Joey bouncing around and waving his arms like a hairy windmill. "Holy smokes! There really was a girl in the boys' locker room! I can't believe it. It's my main squeeze!"

Michelle covered her face as they lifted her into the ambulance. If only the earth would open up and swallow her mortified self, she would die happy.

"You'll be fine, honey," one of the medics said,

misunderstanding her tears. "Your folks are right behind us. We'll be at the hospital in no time."

From the ambulance, Michelle was whisked into the emergency room. There she was finally allowed to sit up so the doctor could check her eyes and ears, bang on her knees, and do a bunch of other important vital-sign stuff—all without commenting on the stiff tufts of gooky hair that were sticking out of her itchy, masking-taped head. But she knew he was looking at it and trying hard not to laugh.

"You act like you've never seen a head wrap before," she said haughtily.

The doctor seemed amused. "Well, no. Not quite like this." He began delicately fingering the edges of Michelle's hairline. "What happens if we take it off?"

From his chair in the corner, Mr. Dupree raised his chin slightly. "Better leave it in place if we can, Doc. It's not going anywhere."

"Yes," her mother agreed. "Apparently, it's not the first time she's had one. Michelle can deal with her so-called head wrap when she gets home."

Gulp. She wasn't out of the woods yet. Maybe she should ask if she could spend the night in the hospital. Before she had a chance, a nurse peeked in the room.

"Your friends called, Michelle. I told them everything is in working order and that you're being released. Oh, by the way, your friends said to make sure you knew that your team won the game."

"Hey, you guys. We creamed the Titans right in their own backyard," Brian yelled. The kitchen door banged behind him. "You think our field is a mess. You should have seen theirs."

Brian stopped in his tracks when he saw Michelle, still in her uniform and with something strange on her head, sandwiched between their parents on the couch.

He blinked and looked again. "What happened to your head?"

"Cool it, Brian. It's masking tape."

"What's going on?"

"That's exactly what we were going to ask you," their father said. "Your sister was shaken up playing football."

Her mother stood up. "Fortunately, she's fine now, but it seems Coach Brown was strangely unaware that he had a girl on his team."

"Huh. Not very observant of him, I'd say."

Mrs. Dupree faced her son. "You knew what was going on weeks ago when you made that big pitch to get Michelle's insurance form signed."

"Hey, I didn't think you'd really mind," Brian said, taking a step backward. "Michelle's being a girl was just a minor detail."

Mrs. Dupree gave him a stern look. "The whole thing was deceitful. You deceived the coach, you deceived the school, and you deceived us. Both of you are in deep, deep trouble."

"But, Brian," Michelle piped up, "you should have seen the moose I took down. It was an awesome play. He was going to score for sure."

Mr. Dupree put his arm around Michelle's shoulder. "What you did was risky, young lady. We're only thankful that you weren't seriously hurt."

"Then everything's okay, Dad?" Michelle said. "Brian and I can still help at the team car wash tomorrow?"

"Car wash?" her mom yelled.

"Mom, get a grip," Brian said. "You remember. It's our one big combo fund-raiser. The high school and junior high teams are raising money to help pay for the field lights. Attendance is mandatory."

"Mandatory, my eyeball! As of right now, both of you are grounded. Indefinitely."

"But, Mom," Michelle whined. "I'm supposed to bring the sponges. I already bought them and everything. I used my whole allowance."

"I'll tell you what you can do with those sponges," she fired back.

Dad cleared his throat while Brian stared at his toes. Michelle couldn't recall when her mother had been so angry. Even Hercules knew to stay out of sight. The poor dog had squeezed into the narrow space between the magazine rack and her dad's recliner. Only the slightest tip of his tail showed.

Thank goodness at that moment the phone rang in the kitchen.

"Yes, Coach Brown. She's doing much better," Michelle heard her mother say. "We're relieved, too." There was a long pause. Michelle leaned forward on the couch.

"Naturally . . . I understand . . . You certainly have a right to your opinion . . . Yes . . . Not really . . . I see . . . Uh-huh . . . Yes, of course there are other sports . . . Excuse me . . . Then the fact that she's a girl . . . Well, in the big picture, isn't Michelle's being a girl a rather minor detail?"

The next pause was much longer.

When her mother resumed talking, her voice was slightly edgy. "Yes, of course, he's home . . . You would . . . Just a minute. Henry, dear!" she called.

Michelle's dad pushed himself off the couch to take the call.

A few minutes later, Mrs. Dupree re-entered the room with her shoulders hunched, arms slack, and knees bowed. She bounced on her feet, snorting and making monkey noises. "Me big Neanderthal coach. You wimpy girl thing. Stay home. Prepare food." She pounded on her chest.

Michelle and Brian cracked up. Anyone who knew Coach Brown would know exactly what she meant.

Mrs. Dupree straightened and looked directly at Michelle. "I've decided you will be the first one at that car wash and you will wash more cars than anyone else. And, Brian," she said, pointing, "you make sure your sister gets the biggest bucket, the sloppiest sponge, and the dirtiest cars. I want her bucket filled at all times. And furthermore, when that chauvinistic coach arrives, you make sure he knows how much work Michelle has done."

"Gee, Brian," Michelle said as they trooped upstairs, followed by a much happier Hercules, "it's going to be nice having my own personal water boy."

Wearing a large yellow T-shirt and blue gym shorts over her bathing suit, Michelle reached down into her bucket and swirled her sponge through the cool water. For the first Saturday in October, it was unseasonably hot. That was okay. In fact, it was perfect, considering this car wash was their only opportunity to raise big bucks to help pay for their night games. The electricity wasn't cheap.

Showing up at the filling station smack in the middle of town for a fund-raiser after the unbelievable embarrassment the night before wasn't exactly easy for Michelle. Only the support she was getting from Matt made it bearable.

He'd called early that morning, waking her.

"You are still coming," he said, not a question.

"My mom's making me."

"Good."

"So what happened after I left the field?" Michelle asked, grateful that Matt never mentioned her masking-taped head wrap. "The last time I saw Coach Brown, he was frothing at the mouth because my helmet popped off and he saw I was a girl instead of a guy. He wasn't the least bit polite to my folks on the phone either. I don't care how he feels, but I do care about the rest of the team."

She'd never heard Matt so wound up. "It was a good thing you tackled that guy as hard as you did. The ball popped right out of his hands and into ours. We had six points on the board in no time. You should have been there, Michelle," he said excitedly. "We were awesome— except for stinko Joey. He missed the extra point by a mile. It was a good thing we didn't need it. Super play, Michelle."

Michelle twisted the cord around her finger and shrugged. "It happened so fast, I didn't have a choice," she said softly.

There was an awkward pause.

"Coach asked me if I knew who you were when you tried out. I didn't want to lie anymore," Matt said finally, stumbling over his words. "But he ought to know we need you. And I know he was glad we won the game."

"Did he say that?" Michelle asked.

"No," Matt was forced to admit. "He was too busy slamming locker doors. Nobody wanted to hang around. We all skipped our showers and left as fast as we could."

"Did the other guys say anything?"

"Sort of." Matt hesitated. "I get the feeling some of them are not too cool about what happened. They're saying Lamar, Rani, and I tricked them by not telling the truth. I think they really feel left out. And, of course, there's Joey. He's totally embarrassed because now the whole school knows that a girl beat him out of the kicking position."

"Is that all?" she asked, suspicious.

"Not exactly," Matt said, sounding embarrassed himself. "A bunch of guys are afraid the other schools will laugh at us for having a girl on the squad."

Michelle took a deep breath. "So how and when do we work this out?"

"At the car wash!" Matt said confidently. "We've got to get it over with as quickly as possible. We're playing the Falcons on Friday, and we can't take up valuable practice time hashing out our differences."

Of course, Matt was right.

A hot October sun beat down on Michelle's back as she squeezed her sponge over the hood of a dusty green Jeep. She was wiping it with a wide circular motion when Sandy startled her from behind.

"Michelle! I was just about to tell you about Skye on the phone this morning when your mom made you hang up. Skye was next to me at the game and when you went down, she practically went into cardiac arrest. Talk about panic. I don't even know CPR! She didn't breathe normally until she found out you were okay. I doubt she slept a wink last night."

"I'll call her later."

"Good idea," Sandy replied, fluffing her ponytail as she looked around. "Is absolutely everyone here? I saw Derek a minute ago. Oooh, this is so neat. Would you just look at Brian and all his high school friends in their tank tops. Whoa!" she said, smacking her lips.

Michelle picked up a brush and went at the tires. She noticed Sandy pull her notebook and purple clicky pen out of her purse.

"Has Jocko wiped out the bake sale yet?" Sandy asked.

Michelle dipped the brush in the bucket and kept scrubbing. A boy Brian knew was on the other side of the Jeep. In another minute or two, they'd have this one finished.

"I haven't seen him yet, but never fear," she said, answering Sandy's question. "Where there's food, Jocko isn't far away."

"Oooh, look who else is here," Sandy squealed as Miss Ashleigh's little red sports car pulled into the filling station.

You would have thought the world was about to end. Every one of the guys stopped squirting and sloshing at the same time. They dropped their bristle brushes and stood there completely awestruck as Miss Ashleigh whirred her window down and extended her perfectly manicured hand.

"Y'all want me to park some place?"

Obviously, it was love at first sight.

Matt was the first to recover. "Sure, Miss Ashleigh. Drive your car over here. I'll wash it." Six other guys elbowed Matt, trying to push him out of the way.

Like it was planned, a lanky photographer in a scruffy purple hat arrived at precisely the same moment.

"Hey, don't I know you from somewhere?" he asked Michelle as he aimed his camera at Miss Ashleigh.

Michelle wiped soap suds off her cheek with the back of her hand and squinted in the bright sun. "I think so. Aren't you from the *Journal*? You took the pictures of our basketball team."

The photographer smiled. "Right. And now you're a cheerleader."

"Nah," Brian said, stepping up. "Michelle's a member

of the football team. She made the winning tackle last night," he said, popping Michelle on the back.

Right away the photographer whipped out his notebook and began scribbling. Sandy's eyes almost bugged out of her head. His notebook was similar to hers.

"A girl on the football team?" the photographer said. "How come nobody told me? Hey, this will make a great lead story."

As Michelle began answering questions, Brian whispered in her ear. "Coach just drove in. Remember what Mom said. Don't talk too long or you'll fall behind." Before wandering off to join the other boys ogling Miss Ashleigh, he squirted more water in Michelle's bucket.

A loud cheer erupted as Coach parked next to the red sports car. His eyes swept the filling station as he checked out the kids from both teams. When his gaze rested on Michelle, standing next to the photographer, it looked like a storm cloud had settled over his head. Then he saw Miss Ashleigh in her bright jogging shorts.

"Hi, y'all," she said, flashing a smile in his direction. "It's a perfect day to get wet." She bent over and opened the car door on the passenger side, indicating the extra goodies she'd brought for the bake sale. "Would you help me tote these sweet things to the booth?"

Sandy giggled as Coach Brown jockeyed with the high school coach for the honor of carrying Miss Ashleigh's cupcakes and cookies to the bake sale table set up on the grassy island on the far side of the filling station.

With her baked goods taken care of, Miss Ashleigh turned to Michelle. "Oh, my dear, I am so pleased to see you are up and around. You simply worried all of us to death last night on the football field."

Michelle blushed. "I'm fine," she said quickly. "The wind got knocked out of me, that's all. They never needed to take me to the hospital."

With all the guys and cheerleaders watching, Miss Ashleigh touched the damp curls that had escaped Michelle's French braid. "Bless your heart. You were just a tiny speck on that stretcher when you passed right below the stands. But I did notice your hair treatment. How clever of you to moisturize your hair under that brutal helmet. How did you come up with such an incredible idea?"

Beside Michelle, Sandy was jumping up and down. "That was my idea."

Miss Ashleigh flashed another smile, this time at Sandy as she turned Michelle's French braid over in her hand. "No wonder her hair bounces so nicely. From now on I'm going to do exactly the same thing when I put on my bicycle helmet."

Michelle heard a titter spread through the cheerleaders. She hoped the people at Wal-Mart were prepared for a run on masking tape.

Out of the corner of her eye, Michelle noticed all the guys going ga-ga. Not one car was being washed. Michelle grimaced. Any second now Coach Brown would return from delivering Miss Ashleigh's baked goodies to the table. The last thing in the world Michelle needed was for him to see or hear her talking girl stuff.

"Gee, thanks, Miss Ashleigh," Michelle said, feeling flattered by all the attention. "But right now we have to make money." She whirled around and hollered. "C'mon, you guys. Get back to work. Matt, I thought you were going to wash Miss Ashleigh's car."

That was when someone sprayed her good with the hose.

She whipped around. It was Jocko Joey in a pukey black-net tank top. Worse, he was making his eyebrows go up and down like a pair of furry black caterpillars. And a stupid grin was spreading across his face like slime.

"Everyone knows why you joined the team," he said loudly. "You couldn't stand not being close to me."

Oh, gag. Michelle groaned, and it wasn't from being drenched.

Apparently, the rest of the team had heard what Joey said.

"Okay, Joey, knock it off," Neil yelled, surprising her.

"Yeah," Tony chimed in. "We're a team."

Michelle could hardly believe her ears.

"Hey, I didn't mean nothing by that," Joey said, backing up.

"Good. Then get past it."

"Yeah. She's a girl, but she's tough."

"And we need her."

Michelle took a deep breath and smiled as Matt stopped washing Miss Ashleigh's car to give her the A-OK sign. She gave him a thumbs-up sign back. With the rest of the team behind her, she could hardly wait for the next practice. No matter what Coach did or said, she was still an Eagle and they were still a team.

But at Monday's practice, Coach Brown shocked everyone.

"I hope you know, you've destroyed my team," he shouted at Michelle. "The only reason I'm keeping you on my roster is because that Title Nine ruling says I have to. So I'm stuck with you."

Michelle gulped at his hostile attitude.

"But I can take you off first string. In my book, someone who signs up using a phony name can't be trusted," he continued. "Furthermore, from this moment on you are to use only regulation equipment at all times. No more hand-me-downs," he said, pounding his clipboard.

Just like that, it was settled, and there was nothing she or any of the others could do about it. Every afternoon before practice, she was to stand outside the boys' locker room to pick up her equipment. But for some mysterious school-policy reason, she wasn't allowed to change in the girls' locker room.

Instead, Coach Brown ordered her to haul everything—helmet, shoulder pads, knee guards, pants, jersey, and cleats, plus her schoolbooks—upstairs to change in the girls' bathroom before walking down the long hall and staircase to join the boys on the field. After practice, when she was sweaty and tired, she had to climb the stairs again, stumble down the hall to the girls' room to change, then haul all her gear back to its place outside the boys' locker room. Sometimes she had to wait as long as fifteen minutes before Coach answered her knock on the door.

She wasn't stupid. She knew he was doing this to show her she wasn't a real part of the team. He wanted to break her spirit. He thought she'd get tired and give up.

But Coach Brown didn't know Michelle Dupree. The nastier he was, the tougher she felt.

He also restricted her to holding for Joey.

By Wednesday, out of boredom, Michelle began catching Matt's passes and running them into the end zone. Coach Brown was livid.

"If you ever get on the field and catch the ball by some stroke of fate, then you are to either signal 'fair catch' or step out of bounds. I will not risk your being injured on my field," Coach Brown yelled loud enough so everyone—team, teachers, cheerleaders, students, and casual passersby—could hear. How humiliating.

"That's not all," Michelle told her family Thursday night at the dinner table. "Coach Brown makes me watch while he lets Joey run the Fire Play."

Mrs. Dupree put her fork down. "I don't think I know that play, Michelle."

"Oh, Mom. It is so neat."

"It's risky," added Brian. "If you lose the ball, nine times out of ten you'll be in a bad field position."

Mr. Dupree nodded at his wife. "That's why we don't know that one."

Michelle leaned forward in her chair. "Yeah, but it is so cool how the other team gets totally faked out expecting you to kick. Instead, the kicker hollers 'fire.' Then everybody runs like crazy, and you can throw the ball to anyone. You might even score."

"I thought only the quarterback could throw the ball."

"Mom! The quarterback isn't even on the field when you kick, you know. Wow!" Michelle said softly. "I would love to run that play. I could, too, if Coach would let me. I have a better throwing arm than Joey." Michelle shook her head in disbelief. "If you ask me, Coach Brown is making a terrible mistake. We play the Falcons tomorrow, and he has me warming the bench and Jocko kicking instead of playing defense."

Brian reached across the table to grab another roll. "Coach Brown is chicken. He's afraid the other coaches will laugh at him. He's not even thinking about the Eagles."

"Well," Michelle said, putting down her milk. "If Coach is afraid of people laughing, he'd better get ready for tomorrow night. Joey is going to make all of us look ridiculous."

"Give me a break," Brian muttered. "Joey can't kick the broad side of a barn when he's standing next to it."

"It's worse than that," Michelle piped. "This afternoon at practice, Joey said he'd seen a video of Joe Montana."

Mrs. Dupree stopped stirring her coffee. "I thought Joe Montana was a quarterback."

"He was," Michelle answered quickly. "But apparently when he played for the Forty-Niners, he held for their kicker. A lot of quarterbacks do. I think Jocko said the kicker's name was Wersching."

"Ray Wersching, a great kicker," Mr. Dupree contributed.

"Right, but superstitious. According to Jocko, Ray Wersching wouldn't look at the goalposts before he kicked. He made Joe Montana lead him out on the field so he wouldn't have to peek. He said looking at the goalposts was the same as looking for bad luck."

"Hmmm," Mr. Dupree mused. "I think I remember reading something about that."

"Yeah," Brian joined in. "Almost all the good players have superstitions. You know I do."

"Well, now Joey thinks it'll be bad luck if he looks at the

goalposts. I tried to talk him out of it, but it didn't work. So tomorrow night, I'm supposed to lead him out on the field. And get this. He says not only is it bad luck to look at the goalposts, it's also bad luck if he looks at the ball!"

"He's going to kick without looking?" Brian almost choked on his milk.

"Yep." Michelle nodded. "With his eyes closed."

Brian put his hand over his face. "Oh, geez."

Mrs. Dupree squeezed her husband's hand. "Darling, this is one game I don't want to miss."

The next evening, just as Coach Brown promised, he started Joey instead of Michelle. The Falcons won the toss and opted to kick off first. As Michelle sat on the bench, Matt led the offense through a successful series of plays, each time achieving another first down.

"Go, Eagles!" Michelle shouted. Eight minutes in the first quarter and they were already on the twenty-five yard line. Out of the corner of her eye, she saw Joey warming up on the sidelines.

Michelle groaned. Oh, please, don't let him go through with it, she said to herself. He must have read her mind. A couple of seconds later, she felt his hand on her right shoulder.

"You ready?" he barked in her ear.

The crowd cheered as Tony ran a screen pass, taking the ball in for six points.

Michelle turned around. Joey had his eyes squeezed tighter than two lemons.

"You got to promise you won't let the laces show."

"What difference does it make?" Michelle growled. "With your eyes shut, you won't be able to see them."

Joey grunted. "It makes a difference. I need all the luck I can get."

Michelle plopped her helmet on and snapped the chin strap. Taking a deep breath, she started slowly toward the seventeen yard line with Joey trailing along behind her.

"Slow down," Joey barked. "I got my eyes closed, remember?"

"How could I possibly forget?"

At the seventeen yard line, Michelle took Joey's hand off her shoulder. With the crowd in stunned silence, she lined him up.

"Okay," she told him. "When I get the ball from the center, I'm going to place it so all you have to do is come straight forward. Three steps. Be sure to start on your left foot."

She crouched down and waited. On the count, Neil snapped the ball between his legs. Expertly, Michelle spun it around and held it in place on the ground with her finger.

Joey started forward—one, two, three hulking steps. He swung his beefy leg, and kicked air.

Oh, my gosh! Now what? She'd never seen this happen in the pro games, and they'd certainly never practiced this play either. Michelle stared at the ball, still secure under her finger. Meanwhile, Joey was running in the opposite direction, yelping like a spoiled puppy. What was she supposed to do?

Michelle did the only thing she could think of. She cradled the ball securely in her arms and fell on it. Then every one of the Falcons piled on top of her. By the time the referees pulled all the guys off, she felt like a wet noodle.

"What are you trying to do to me?" Joey yelled at her as the kicking team left the field. "You moved the ball."

"What happened?" Matt demanded.

Michelle adjusted her shoulder pads with an angry jerk. "What are you asking me for? Ask Jocko. And then ask our stupid coach why he's putting up with that clown."

Matt must have understood her frustration. Right away he calmed down. "Don't worry," he said, patting her on the shoulder. "I'll take care of it. Jocko won't try that trick again."

But he did—four more times before the final whistle blew. The Eagles lost 28 to 6. Even worse, when Michelle and the rest of the Eagles went to congratulate the Falcons at the end of the game, most of them were doubled up with laughter.

"The Eagles aren't a team anymore," Michelle told Sandy on the way home. "We're a joke."

The whole time she ranted and raved and vented her frustration, Sandy either clicked her purple clicky pen or wrote in her notebook.

The next day was Saturday. Mr. and Mrs. Dupree needed Brian and Michelle to help them at the store with their annual inventory.

"It's really funny," Michelle said, as she organized the beverage glasses according to size. "At first I didn't like the idea of making the team as a boy. But then, when I did such a good job punting and kicking, it was really cool to be part of the team. Girl or boy, it didn't matter. Now everyone knows I'm a girl, but it shouldn't be a big deal. I'm still a good kicker—far better than Joey. So why won't Coach play me?"

Brian was standing on a ladder, color-coding boxes of balloons. "I told you. Coach Brown is afraid the other coaches will laugh at him."

"Of all the Neanderthal, chauvinistic . . ." Mrs. Dupree mumbled under her breath as she moved the silver punch bowls to a higher shelf.

"But I can't be more hilarious than Joey," Michelle said. "At least I keep my eyes open."

Mr. Dupree set a box of fresh doughnuts on the counter along with several cartons of juice. He motioned everyone to dig in.

"We were there and we understand, sweetheart," he said. "There's only one possible explanation. Coach Brown didn't play you because you're a girl. And if I'm not mistaken, that's illegal."

Mrs. Dupree pushed the punch bowls farther back on the shelf. "I'm calling him," she shouted angrily over her shoulder. "Enough of this speculation. How dare that man treat our family like this!" She stepped down off the stool. "Henry, give me the phone book." She stood at the counter and grabbed the phone, then began punching the numbers. "Someone needs to set that man straight."

CHAPTER 12

Groaning, Michelle climbed on the late bus and plopped in the empty seat in front of Sandy and Skye. "Coach has me kicking again."

"You don't sound very happy about it," Skye said.

Michelle scowled. "My timing's off and I can't kick worth a darn," she complained. "Last week I was only allowed to hold for jerky Jocko. Now my muscles have completely atrophied."

"I've got muscle bomb left over from basketball," Skye offered. "Joe Namath stuff."

"Balm," Michelle corrected. "Thanks, but even Joe Namath couldn't help."

"Wow. That is bad."

"Pooh! You think you've got problems," Sandy said. "All you have to do is kick the ball and everyone knows you're a natural. Poor me. *I've* got to write about it. What's worse, now that Ms. Cramer is constantly raving about my gripping copy, she expects every article to be Pulitzer material. It's all your fault, Michelle."

"Me?" Michelle blew a puff of air upward to cool her

forehead. "How do you figure that?"

"Because you've been my advising editor from the very beginning," Sandy exclaimed.

Skye laughed. "It's a good thing. That story you wrote about Neil's hikey was hysterical. Even I knew the guy in the center *hikes* the ball."

"Close enough," Sandy said defensively. "The problem is, Ms. Cramer isn't giving me assignments anymore. She says now that I've proven myself, I'm free to come up with my own ideas. Oh, the pressure of it all! So many choices and so little time. What do you think I should write about?"

No one said anything for a moment. Then Skye piped up, "What about food? You could ask everyone on the team what they eat to give them the winning edge."

"Hmmm, Eagle Eating, Football Food, Confidential Calories," Sandy mused. "A triple headline. That does have possibilities."

Especially if Sandy interviewed guys with pregame eating habits similar to Brian's, Michelle thought with a smile.

"Okay," Sandy said. "Now how can we solve your problem, Michelle? Football can't be the only thing bothering you."

Michelle put her head back and slumped farther down in the seat. "Oh, you know. The boys are saying my mom ragged Coach. Now they hate me. Even Matt."

"Matt?" Sandy shrieked. "Impossible."

Michelle nodded miserably. "This afternoon when Joey kept calling me Super Shank, Matt didn't even come to my defense. That's a depressing first."

"Gosh, no exaggeration," Skye whispered. "You sound

121

like your heart might break. I'm so sorry, Michelle."

Sandy hunched forward, her eyebrows knit together. "Wow, dissension in the ranks. This could be a real scoop." She whipped her notebook and her purple clicky pen out of her purse. "I think I could handle that."

Michelle shook her head vigorously. "You can't write about that!" she said. "What I told you was a secret. You know, off the record."

Skye agreed. "You have to report on what you see in the game, unless it's an interview or something. Write about food. That way, you'll get to interview more guys."

The wheels turning in Sandy's head were clearly visible in her eyes. "Yeah, you're right," she said, putting her clicky pen away. "I already have some of their phone numbers memorized."

The next day, things didn't get any better for Michelle. She woke up late and blew a fuse when she tried to use the hair dryer while making toast. She hollered at Hercules when he failed to fetch her sports bra from the laundry basket. Then, feeling badly, she buried her face in his golden ruff and cried, which only made her mascara run. When her mom drove her to school on her way to the shop, they hit every red light. And then, when her mom let her out in front of the school, Michelle stepped in a puddle. Now her shoes would squeak all day. Why was she not surprised that the bell had already rung, which meant she had to report to the office? Why was she not shocked when she opened her locker, only to have all her belongings tumble into the hallway? Why was she not as startled as the rest of her classmates when their math teacher announced a pop quiz for which she was totally unprepared?

By mid-morning, Michelle was desperate for something to go right. She hurried down the hall to Teen Living as fast as her squeaky shoes would carry her, hoping that her favorite teacher would chase away the storm clouds and bring on the sun.

But when she hurried into cooking and saw the poem written in big, bold letters on the chalkboard, Michelle stopped dead in her tracks. Her jaw went limp and her throat felt dry.

> *Roses are red,*
> *Violets are blue.*
> *Boys in the locker room,*
> *And a tomboy, too!*

She was still standing there in complete humiliation, the public joke of Jefferson Junior High, when Miss Ashleigh finally entered her classroom.

"Why, what on earth is this? An early Valentine?" she said, walking up to the chalkboard. She placed a perfectly manicured finger to her cheek. "Oh, it's poetry, and not very polite either. Well, my folks always told me if I couldn't say something nice, I shouldn't say anything at all. I think it's a good lesson for all of you. I'll ignore this," she said as she picked up the eraser and looked over her shoulder. "This time."

Michelle found her place at the table beside Matt. He should have erased the poem before she saw it.

Later that evening, Brian was in his room, supposedly

doing his homework, when Michelle offered him a brownie. She'd baked them using the recipe from cooking class.

Suddenly, Brian lurched forward, his eyes wide with pain. His hand went to his jaw. "Ouch! I think I cracked a tooth." He turned the chocolate square over, examining it. "This isn't a brownie. It's a chocolate brick!"

"Fine," Michelle yelled. "Give it back!"

So he did. He threw it at her.

The brownie hit the wall behind Michelle with a clunk and dropped to the floor, intact. Brian loved it.

"Did you see that?" he whooped. "Artillery!"

Suddenly, Michelle burst into uncontrollable, racking sobs.

"Mom!" Brian leaped off the bed, ran to the door, and yelled. "Something's wrong with Michelle!"

Michelle raced across the hall and slammed her bedroom door. Then she buried her head in Hercules's neck and, for the second time that day, sobbed her heart out. She had almost finished crying when her mother tapped on her door.

"Come on in. It's open."

"Michelle, are you all right?" her mother asked softly. "Is there anything I can do?"

Michelle sniffed. "You could start by making me quit the team."

Mrs. Dupree wrapped her arms around Michelle's shoulders. "I don't think you mean that, sweetie. Has Coach Brown done something else?"

"No, Mom. You don't understand!" Michelle moaned. "It's not Coach's rotten attitude or how I have to traipse through the school carrying armloads of gear and books just to get dressed and undressed. I can handle that. But everyone's watching me now—kids, parents, the other teams, even the photographer from the *Journal*. They're going to make fun of me because I'm kicking so bad. This afternoon when Joey held the ball, every single one of my attempts was a complete disaster. You'd think I'd never put my foot to pigskin in my entire life. Even Matt's disappointed in me. He doesn't have to say it. I can tell. I'm letting everyone down."

"Can't anybody help you with kicking?" Mom asked. "Isn't that the coach's job?"

"He doesn't know how," Michelle wailed. "*Nobody* knows how. They just say, 'Go out and kick the ball.' It's not like the pros. There's no such thing as a kicking coach in junior high. I'm supposed to kick the ball, and like magic it's supposed to sail between the uprights."

"Oh, Michelle."

"The problem is," Michelle continued, "I must be practicing all wrong, because the ball never goes between the uprights."

"You did it right before. I'm certain whatever you were doing will come back."

"But when, Mom? I can't wait forever. We play the Washington Generals on Friday. And the game after that is with the Barracudas."

"Mom, what's the matter with Michelle?" Brian whispered from the doorway. "I was only kidding about the brownie." He had a really concerned look on his face. "I was even going to ask for seconds. I could suck on it for a while. Maybe mush it in milk . . ."

Michelle's shoulders shook as she tried to catch her breath and regain her composure.

"Your sister's worried about Friday's game, not brownies."

"Oh, that's all." Brian's face brightened. "Hey, Michelle, no sweat. The Generals are real pushovers. You and the Eagles will walk all over those guys."

Michelle took another deep breath. "That's easy for you to say. Friday is an away game. I'll be in enemy territory, the only girl in the entire division. They'll be whistling and calling me names."

Brian tapped his mother's arm. "Maybe I should go to the game, Mom. I could sit on the Washington side. They wouldn't dare do anything to Michelle then."

Mrs. Dupree shook her head. "Brian, you have your own game. Your father and I will go. Michelle will be fine."

"Okay, but if you change your mind . . ."

Michelle wiped her nose with a tissue and tried to smile. Saturday she'd bake a double batch of brownies. Lucky Brian!

"Good news, Michelle! Hot off the press!" Sandy announced Thursday in the cafeteria. "I got permission to ride the team bus to tomorrow's game."

"Great," Skye said enthusiastically. "I'm going with the Pep Squad. I'll meet you there."

Sandy sat down and opened her lunch bag. "Just think of it," she gushed to everyone within earshot. "Me, Michelle, and all those hunky football players. Eat your hearts out, girls! I haven't been able to crash the boys' locker room yet, but I'm on my way."

"Great article in *The Lantern*." A girl Michelle recognized from math class stopped by to congratulate

Sandy on yesterday's edition. "Thanks to your analysis, I finally understand the game."

"Do you want me to autograph it for you?" Sandy had her clicky pen ready. "Wait until you read my next piece. It's an exclusive on our team's fabulous food intake." She opened the newspaper to the sports page. "Now I just have to come up with something equally terrific for next week."

Michelle watched as Sandy signed her name with an i instead of a y and dotted it with a heart.

"I'm not worried." Sandy winked at Michelle. "I'm sure to get an exclusive on the bus."

It was enough to make Michelle retch. She reached inside Sandy's lunch bag and pulled out a marshmallow, then stuck it in Sandy's mouth.

She and Skye had to hang on to their sides, they laughed so hard.

Coach Brown wanted the Eagles on the team bus by five-thirty. Michelle, Sandy, boys, and coaches bounced along curvy country roads before arriving at Washington Junior High some forty-five minutes later. The whole time Sandy had been a nonstop clicky-pen chatterbox. She'd gathered enough quotes to fill three notebooks, and that was just from listening to Coach. By the time they climbed off the bus, Michelle doubted Coach Brown would ever allow Sandy on his bus again. Michelle might even have to sneak her friend on for the return trip!

But with Sandy happily tossing her ponytail and babbling away beside her, Michelle had almost forgotten about the game. She smiled at Matt sitting near Lamar, Neil, and Rani. She wasn't one bit worried about field goals or extra points. It was like they were on a school outing, all laughs and good times.

Then the driver pulled into enemy territory and opened the doors with a rubber-lipped *whoosh*.

Gulp. If only this were a dream and Michelle would wake up. Instead, carrying an armload of gear, she stepped onto the curb.

"You must be the new Eagles kicker I read about in the *Journal*," a lady teacher greeted her. "I'll show you to the bathroom so you can change."

"Bye, you handsome hunks! See you later." Sandy waved her notebook as she trotted after Michelle.

Michelle groaned. *Handsome hunks?* Why couldn't Sandy understand? Football was serious business. She and the rest of the team had work to do.

The two girls followed the teacher down a hall and around a corner to the bathroom. When she pushed the heavy door open, the Washington girls inside stopped talking and stared. There was only silence coupled with an occasional flush.

By the time they reached the field, Coach Brown already had the rest of the Eagles doing their warm-up exercises. Quickly, Michelle found her place. She began touching her toes and doing windmills. While the others began passing the ball and knocking into each other's shoulders, she swung her leg to loosen the muscles. Then she set up the practice net and began kicking the ball into it.

The sun was beginning to set when Michelle saw her parents chatting with Sandy. A few minutes later, the Generals kicked off to the Eagles. Tony caught the ball on the thirty-five yard line, running it twenty-five yards.

It didn't take long to realize that the Generals were every bit as awful as Brian had predicted. Matt and the Eagles' offense were steamrolling down the field.

Matt tossed another long pass, a completion. As the lights snapped on, the Eagles cheerleaders began jumping up and down and waving their blue-and-gold pom-poms.

"Yea, Matt!"

Four minutes into the game and the Eagles had already put six points on the board.

The few Eagles fans stood up, cheering. Someone was ringing a lonely cowbell. With a gulp, Michelle picked up her helmet as boys ran off the field and the kicking unit ran on. Smooth as clockwork, Neil hiked the ball expertly to Jocko, who placed it squarely on the ground. Michelle took a deep breath and began her approach. Three steps and her toe caught the ball, shanking it about a mile to the right.

The laughs were deafening.

"Tune it out. It'll be better next time," Matt encouraged her as she came off the field.

"Sure," she mumbled, wanting badly to believe him.

The Eagles were ahead at halftime 36–0. They swarmed toward the locker room, patting each other on the back and grinning widely—all except Michelle. She couldn't go with the boys, and having missed every kick, she had nothing to smile about.

During the second half, Coach put everyone in the game. They worked almost all the plays from their playbook and invented a few new ones. It seemed nothing could go wrong—except when it was time for Michelle to kick.

The final score was 54–0 and might have gone higher

except the referees mercifully called the game at the end of the third quarter. Matt had led the Eagles to nine touchdowns, but Michelle hadn't made one extra point.

Thank goodness the ride back into town was a dark one. Nobody on the bus could see Michelle's red nose or bloodshot eyes. Of course, the rest of the team, revved up by their win, probably wouldn't have noticed. Even so, Michelle was glad to have her best friend sitting next to her for moral support.

"I played awful," Michelle whined, leaning close so Sandy could hear. "This slump is the pits. My punts were okay, and my kickoffs certainly were long enough. But I haven't kicked a ball between the goalposts in so long, I forget what it feels like."

"At least we still won. Who are we playing next week?" Sandy asked.

"The Barracudas."

"Yikes."

"Yeah, with the Barracudas, every point counts. What am I going to do? I've got to get my kick back."

Neither girl said anything for a long time.

Finally, Sandy said, "Maybe I could ask Ms. Cramer to talk Coach Brown into letting me attend all the practices."

Michelle nodded. "Could you?"

Sandy showing moral support at her practices might be exactly what she needed to bring her out of her slump. Anyway, it couldn't hurt.

A few minutes later, Michelle glanced at Sandy as some bright lights shone through the bus window. Her friend appeared to be deep in thought as she rhythmically tapped her pen on the cover of her notebook.

For once, Sandy was mysteriously quiet.

130

CHAPTER 13

Michelle's lower lip quivered as she read the headline screaming across the top of *The Lantern*'s sports page. KICKER KLUNKS. Quickly she scanned the article Sandy had written. Her name jumped off the page five times! Words like *slump, shank,* and *failed attempts* struck her to the core. How could her best friend betray her like this—especially in her time of need?

Michelle had picked up *The Lantern* as she'd left Teen Living. Sandy's was the first article she'd turned to. Number one, Sandy was her best friend, so she was naturally interested. Number two, this week's assignment was the first Sandy had written without her expert assistance. Michelle had thought it was peculiar that Sandy hadn't asked for her help. Now she knew why.

Sandy hadn't been showing her undying support. She was too busy preparing to stab her best friend in the back with her obnoxious purple clicky pen.

With a loud slam, Michelle shut her locker and gave the combination lock a fast twirl. Seething, she gritted her teeth and stormed toward the cafeteria. Sandy was a traitor of the worst sort. Never in a million years would Michelle ever trust that forked-tongued writing reptile again.

Michelle's regular place at the table with Sandy and Skye was waiting, as if nothing traumatic had happened. It could have been any other day the way Sandy was fluffing her ponytail as she talked with Skye. Recalling the article's choice phrases, Michelle faced the truth. Sandy had the conscience of a lowly slug.

Michelle seized a tray off the stack and moved up the line. She pointed to the first things she saw without observing how appetizing they were. Shriveled reheated fish sticks found their way onto her tray, as did soft squishy peas and runny orange Jell-O on a wilted lettuce leaf. When the cafeteria lady gave her two spoonfuls of creamed broccoli with green lumps, Michelle didn't even flinch. Fortunately, the cashier, smiling kindly, stuck a bright yellow banana beside the Jell-O. But Michelle was far too busy obsessing over KICKER KLUNKS to care.

Still clutching *The Lantern* in her hand, she barely managed to balance her tray as she eased through the jostling crowd. Sandy was completely absorbed, talking to the Pep Squad members sitting across from her. Skye saw her first. Her eyes widened as she noticed Michelle's cafeteria lunch. "Wow! Green lumps and fish. What were you thinking?"

Michelle dropped her tray on the table beside Sandy with a loud thud. Everyone at the table stared at her, completely dumbfounded, as she rattled *The Lantern* in Sandy's startled face.

"Look, Miss Sandy-with-a-y-not-an-i-dotted-with-a-heart Vacaro, what I told you was supposed to be private! You and your mighty purple clicky pen had no business

132

blabbing to the whole world! In case it didn't occur to you, what you wrote was *miserable* writing. It wasn't even accurate."

"What I wrote was the truth," Sandy retorted. "And in case *you* didn't know, I have an obligation to my readers. Besides, all the kids at the Generals game saw how you muffed every kick."

A Pep Squad girl leaned forward. "Leave Sandy alone. She's right. It's all everyone's been talking about."

Michelle didn't need to hear that. "Oh, yeah?" she said, gritting her teeth. Her face had reached the boiling point. "I don't remember inviting you into this conversation."

Four Pep Squad members scrambled from their chairs.

Michelle turned back to Sandy. "You're supposed to be my friend. How could you write about me like that?"

"Well, excuse me!" Sandy said snidely. "As long as you're doing well, I can write about super kicker Michelle Dupree kicking the ball from goalpost to goalpost and winning the game with absolutely no help from anyone else. But if you're messing up, I'm supposed to look the other way and act like it never happened. What kind of reporting is that? It's lousy reporting," Sandy answered her own question. "And I'm not going to do it. Not for my best friend and not for anyone else. Besides," Sandy added, "Skye read it before I turned it in. She didn't see anything wrong with my story. Did you, Skye?"

Michelle blinked. Stunned, she faced Skye.

"She did have a couple of words misspelled."

"Except for that," Sandy persisted.

Michelle grabbed a carrot stick from Skye's lunch. "I can't believe what Sandy said about me didn't bother you."

Skye blushed. "Actually, Michelle, you *didn't* make those kicks," she said shyly. "Pardon me for saying so, but maybe you shouldn't be playing. You almost got yourself killed once. It could happen again, you know." She paused. "I never thought you should play football in the first place. That's why I left the note in Coach Brown's locker."

For a moment, the world stood still. "You did what?"

"I left a note in Coach's locker. But I never mentioned your name."

Michelle shook her head. "Coach doesn't have a locker."

"Yes, he does," Skye insisted. "I saw it for myself when I snuck in the locker room. It's the biggest locker—the first one with the Power Rangers decal."

"That's Jocko Joey's." Suddenly, a light went on in Michelle's head. "The note about who let more girls in the boys' locker room—you wrote it! I can't believe it. I just can't," Michelle mumbled. "I've been betrayed by my two best friends. Why on earth would you do such a thing?"

Skye's voice quivered. "I told you, I didn't want you to get hurt. I still don't. I thought if Coach knew there was a girl on the team, he'd make you quit. I never expected your parents would let you play. Who would? And I never thought you'd be fighting with me and Sandy either. I wish we'd never gone to watch the boys play football that day. This is turning into one huge mess!"

"Oh, for pete's sake." Michelle stuffed her banana in her purse. "You two deserve each other. Here!" She shoved her tray in the middle of the table. "Eat my lunch!"

The Eagles' final practice before the big game against the Barracudas was brutal, emotionally and physically. Coach kept Matt busy in offensive drills and passing patterns. He had Jocko playing left tackle, which left Michelle by herself. While the rest of the team worked diligently on their plays, Michelle tediously lined footballs up in the grass at the far end of the field. She backed up precisely behind each ball, made her routine approach, and fired away. Surprisingly enough, a couple of balls actually wobbled between the uprights. Not enough to make Michelle relax, but enough to give her a rare smidgen of hope.

Once, when the ball hit the crossbar and toppled over, she glanced back in Coach Brown's direction. She thought she saw a trace of a smile. But he returned to writing plays on his clipboard before she could be sure.

More than anything, she wished she could talk to Matt or any of the guys—except Joey. She needed to get revved up, but she never had a chance. Maybe she would phone Matt when she got home.

Matt picked up the phone on the second ring.

"Oh, hi, Michelle. I saw you kick a couple of good ones today. Sorry I didn't get to tell you. The guys are sort of giving me a hard time. Coach knows it and he expects me to be the leader. It isn't easy."

"No kidding," Michelle agreed. "They're giving me a hard time, too. It's like they wished I'd never tried out, even Lamar and Rani. You, too, probably. I'm kind of surprised Sandy didn't quote you saying something bad about me in *The Lantern*."

"Maybe it's because I didn't give her anything juicy enough." Matt laughed. "I did like the article though."

"You did? Even the headline?"

"What headline?"

"Kicker Klunks!"

"I didn't even notice that. I meant the stuff about me—quarterback Matt Peterson steamrolling the Eagles into Generals territory." Matt sounded remarkably like a Monday-night football commentator. "Sandy sure has a way with words. She made us sound so tough. Ms. Cramer should make her editor next year."

"I can't believe my ears. You're on her side, too." She started to rant and rave, but was stopped immediately by Matt's shouting.

"Michelle!" Matt yelled into the phone. "You knew playing football would be hard. You knew playing as a girl would be four times harder. Come on. Snap out of it. We've got our biggest game tomorrow."

"I know that, QB. Why do you think I called? Don't you think I know how we need every point against the Barracudas? What if I mess up again?"

"Maybe if you concentrated," Matt suggested.

"I am concentrating."

"Then maybe if you didn't concentrate," he said, which was absolutely no help at all. She was about to tell him so when he continued. "Maybe you're getting too tense, worrying about it. If I didn't know better, I'd think you were deliberately messing up your kicks by kicking off the laces."

136

"What? Wait a second. What did you say about laces?" Michelle asked. "I *am* kicking off the laces—sometimes. I mean, I'm not trying not to. That would be superstitious."

"Who told you that?"

"Jocko."

"Joey?" Matt exploded. "Man, I'll cream that bozo. Wait till I tell Coach."

"Why? What's the matter?"

"Michelle! Kicking off the laces makes the ball go kaflooey. That skunk was sabotaging your kicks. I thought something was strange when your punts were okay. The only time the ball went wild was when Joey was holding. I'm definitely calling Coach."

"No!" Michelle shrieked. "He must be sick of getting phone calls about me. First my mom and now you. Besides, when you tell him I was kicking off the laces, I'll look dumb."

"No, you won't," Matt argued. "Who would expect someone who never played football before to know an intricate detail like that?"

"I still say don't call. What if you tell him and I continue to mess up? It'll look like I'm trying to make excuses. Coach will think I'm a stupid crybaby—a girl who doesn't know any better. Besides, Joey will only deny it. Nobody would believe me."

For a few seconds neither of them said anything.

Suddenly, Matt said, "Hey, I know. I'll hold for you in the game. A lot of quarterbacks do. Coach will probably keep Joey busy on defense anyway. I'm coming right over. We've got to beat the Barracudas tomorrow. This might be the only way."

The Duprees made it a family affair. Mr. Dupree turned

137

the spotlights on in the driveway while Mrs. Dupree directed the flashlight on the ball. While Hercules lay in the cool grass alongside the driveway, Brian hiked the ball to Matt, who placed it on the ground for Michelle. Each time she kicked the ball straight as an arrow and squarely over the garage—exactly between the chimney and the TV antenna—everyone jumped and cheered.

"I'd say this calls for hot buttered popcorn and cider," Mrs. Dupree announced as she started for the kitchen door.

"Perfect." Mr. Dupree rubbed his hands together. "Herc and I will get the balls."

Gosh, Michelle thought to herself. This was almost like a date. At least it could count as a rehearsal. Her mother better remember to give them napkins. Matt might want to hold her hand.

Oh, my gosh! Michelle thought in panic. Was she supposed to tell Matt if his hands were greasy? What if some popcorn stuck in her teeth? Would Brian call her Garbage Mouth in front of Matt? She would absolutely die. Michelle had never read as many teen magazines as Sandy, but surely you weren't supposed to use words like *garbage* on a date.

In a daze, Michelle floated into the empty family room. Oh, no! Where was she supposed to sit? Except for Brian, she'd never sat on a couch with a boy before. But what else was left? Nobody sat in her father's recliner. If she sat on the floor beside the coffee table and Matt sat on the couch with Brian, she'd be staring at Matt's knees. But if Matt sat on the floor and she was on the couch with Brian, Matt would be staring at *her* knees! Besides, she didn't think girls were supposed to sit next to their brothers on a date, even if it was only a rehearsal.

Michelle was beginning to understand why some people never got married. It was too hard trying to figure out where to sit.

Just then the phone rang. Great! Michelle breathed a sigh of relief as she doubled back to the kitchen to take the call. When it came to boy-girl things, Sandy always knew what to do. But the call was for Michelle's father. Then she remembered. She and Sandy had had a fight.

Meanwhile, in the family room, at least one problem was solved. Brian was sitting on the floor drinking cider while Matt sat on the couch. Michelle perched on the arm of the couch and took a sip of cider while their parents finished washing the dinner dishes in the kitchen.

A few minutes later, Matt wiped his hands on a napkin and politely scooped his smaller bowl into the larger one for more buttered popcorn. "I heard what you said to Sandy yesterday at lunch," he said. "That was pretty mean. After all, she is supposed to be your best friend."

"Was," Michelle corrected. She reached inside her knapsack and passed a crumpled copy of *The Lantern* to Brian. "Here, read this garbage." Oops! She'd used the *G* word. "Sandy had no business writing this awful stuff about me," she quickly added.

When he finished reading, Brian wiped the butter off his mouth with the back of his hand. He licked his lips and belched. "Get real, Michelle. It looks to me like Sandy was doing her job. This article isn't about you. You're only in five lines. The rest is about Matt and the other guys. I think it's good. I wish we had a sports writer like Sandy. I'd like her to write something about me and our team."

Brothers! Michelle thought in disgust.

CHAPTER 14

A fight with her best friend felt lonely, like the time Hercules had to spend the whole night at the vet's and Michelle wasn't allowed to call him to say good night. Without Herc around, Michelle didn't feel like herself. Without Sandy, she didn't feel right either.

Michelle had wanted to call Sandy after Matt left, but by the time Brian got off the phone with someone named Alma, it was too late.

Michelle pictured herself apologizing to Sandy at the bus stop. Sandy would say that she was sorry, too. Then they would talk about glamour do's and don'ts, what teacher smelled like cigarettes and mouthwash, and, by the way, did you know that Matt came over to my house last night to hang out? By the time they arrived at Jefferson, everything would be back to normal.

But Sandy wasn't at the bus stop the next morning. Riding to school, there was no one to apologize to or chatter with about magazines, teachers, or Matt. Michelle could only stare idly out the window and worry about the Barracudas. Surrounded by loads of rambunctious kids, Michelle walked into school a lonely girl.

If the Pep Squad had shown their spirit by decorating the school before the other games, this time they had gone berserk. There was not an inch of bare wall space. With banners and slogans hanging everywhere, including the girls' bathroom, the school swirled in shades of blue and gold. In the library, a mannequin dressed in an Eagles uniform held a shiny inflatable rubber shark—it was supposed to be a Barracuda—firmly in place with his foot. SQUASH THE BARRACUDAS. BIOGRAPHIES IN AISLE 6 the sign read. Hearts dotted the *i*'s. That definitely had Sandy's touch!

Every time the bell rang, Michelle dashed into the hall, hoping to bump into Sandy, but she never did. Then, halfway through math class, someone dropped a note folded in the shape of a football on Michelle's desk. Startled, Michelle jerked backward in her chair. Her fingers itched to unfold the piece of paper. The note had to be from Sandy! Smiling confidently to herself, Michelle hunched over her desk when the teacher wasn't looking.

Oh, a note from Matt.

> *Michelle—I talked to Coach. He said okay but*
> *he wants to check us out on the field before the*
> *pep rally. See you in T.L. Matt.*

"So, did you get my note?" Matt asked when he caught up with Michelle outside of Teen Living. Michelle hugged her books closer to her chest. She was standing beside the water fountain, anxiously waiting to see Sandy before her sewing class.

"Yeah. What did you do about Jocko?" she asked.

"I went to Coach."

"Matt!" Michelle's voice dropped to a hoarse whisper. She stepped aside so Lamar could get a drink. "That's not what we discussed."

"It's okay, okay?" Matt answered. "Coach is the one who brought it up. He asked me if I would hold. He's concerned that maybe Joey isn't placing the ball tight enough against the ground. That would account for the shanks."

"Huh," Lamar said, wiping his mouth. "How did Coach get so smart all of a sudden? He never paid attention to Michelle's kicking before."

Matt shrugged.

"Hello, Michelle," Skye greeted her cheerfully. "What are you doing out here? The bell's going to ring any minute."

"Waiting for Sandy. Have you seen her?"

Skye brushed her long blond hair over her shoulder. "I thought you knew. She's helping with the pep rally—cutting classes like crazy. She's even skipping lunch." Skye shook her head in distress. "Very unhealthy if you ask me."

"That's precisely why I want you boys and girls in my cooking class learning about proper nutrition," Miss Ashleigh said as she swished past them in a long floral skirt, her high heels clicking on the tiled floor. She beckoned everyone inside and directed them to their cooking stations.

"Y'all are going to have the best time tonight pulverizing those Barracuda people," Miss Ashleigh drawled. "I plan to be on the fifty yard line watching it happen. If you see me, I want you to come right up and say 'hey.'"

Matt and the other boys grinned from ear to ear and blushed like their hearts were on fire.

Skye glanced at Michelle. "Say hey?"

"Y'all are just so lucky to have such a fine school," Miss Ashleigh went on. "Why, my junior high played football in a big old cow pasture. Of course, we had an offense and defense. But most importantly, we had a cleanup squad. They went on the field before we could play, if you get my drift."

Michelle and the others chuckled.

"What about practice?" someone from the back of the room asked.

"Well, sometimes the squad didn't clean up as good as they should have and we suffered because of it."

"Oh, gross," the guys roared. The girls pinched their noses.

"Another thing we did have," Miss Ashleigh continued, "was plenty of coaches. That's such a nice thing about the South, you know. Football is very important there."

"Doesn't sound like it, if you had to play in a cow pasture," a snooty girl said, giggling.

Miss Ashleigh shook her finger. "Excuse me, missy. I'll have you know by the time I graduated from college, my alma mater high school had a football stadium that would turn your eyes green," Miss Ashleigh said proudly. "Bleachers clear up to the sky and filled every Friday night. You never knew if you might be rooting for a future Heisman trophy winner. We had our share, you know."

Michelle raised her hand. "Did you ever play?"

Miss Ashleigh perched on a stool and crossed her legs. "No. Not that I didn't want to, but my forte lay in cheerleading. My brother played, though. He was the kicker. And I'll tell you, I know kicking is not easy."

Michelle blinked back the tears. What a nice thing for a former cheerleader to say, and in front of the whole

143

class, too. If everyone hadn't been watching, she would have hugged Miss Ashleigh on the spot.

During her afternoon classes, Michelle stared at the clock until she thought its metal hands might melt. Finally, thirty minutes before the scheduled pep rally, she handed her teacher an official pass and headed for her locker.

She reached the athletic field ahead of Matt, but Coach wasn't alone. He was standing on the sidelines, his shoulders thrown back and chest puffed up like a peacock's. Michelle blinked. He was talking to Miss Ashleigh!

Michelle couldn't tear her eyes away from the startling twosome. She'd never seen anyone approach Coach Brown quite like this. Miss Ashleigh was looking up at the coach and talking right in his face, and Coach seemed to be enjoying every minute of it. Once in a while, when the wind billowed Miss Ashleigh's skirt around her long legs, she would reach up with one hand to hold her blond curls out of her upturned face. The smell of her fragrance was everywhere.

Sandy would never believe it. Coach Neanderthal under Miss Ashleigh's spell? Amazing! Feeling awkward, Michelle held her helmet against her hip and hung back until Miss Ashleigh saw her.

"Why, Michelle Dupree! If it isn't my favorite little Eagle."

Taking a deep breath, Michelle trotted over to stand beside the beautiful young teacher.

"Now, you listen to your coach, Michelle. He is so inspiring with his clever ideas." Miss Ashleigh draped her arm across Michelle's shoulders. "Aren't you, Charlie?"

When *Charlie* agreed and swaggered off toward the goal line, Miss Ashleigh winked at Michelle.

A short time later, Coach snapped the ball to Matt, who twirled it expertly so the laces were facing forward, away from Michelle. In less than a heartbeat, Matt placed the ball solidly on the tee at the correct angle.

Michelle began her approach. Her foot connected.

"All right!" Matt whooped as the ball sailed between the uprights.

"Yes!" Michelle's hands covered her mouth. She bounced on her toes in pure delight.

Hopefully, she would do as well during tonight's game against the Barracudas.

"Mom!" Michelle shouted. "Have you seen my socks? You didn't wash them, did you? I need them stiff so they'll stay up."

In all the years she'd had Brian for a brother, she never thought she'd say that. But it was the truth. Clean, her athletic socks felt too soft. Dirty, or at least worn twice, they had a more aggressive feel.

"Brian!" her mom yelled back. "Did you see your sister's socks when you put the laundry away?"

"Nope," Brian hollered.

"Hercules!" Brian and Michelle both yelled at once.

Like the prince that he was, Hercules disappeared underneath Michelle's bed and returned with both socks in his mouth. Wagging his tail proudly, he dropped them at her feet.

"Thanks, Herc," she said, ruffling his fur. Now her socks were not only grubby, they were also moist with doggie drool. Perfect! She threw the socks in her bag and started for the stairs. It was time to go to the game.

As always, Michelle suited up in the girls' bathroom. When she tapped on the boys' locker room door, Rani let her in. "Ah, good. It's important that you be here for this meeting. It is not negotiable."

Michelle stepped past Rani. The team was gathered around Coach as he drew X's and O's on the chalkboard, going over the game plan she'd heard repeated a hundred times this week.

Since little of it applied to her, Michelle began doing her stretching exercises. First some toe touches, and then some windmills, followed by a calf wall stretch. Finally, she sat down on the floor beside the laundry cart and got serious. Ten straight leg hangs, followed by side-to-side splits. She sat with one leg straight out and the other tucked under, then lowered her chest to her thigh for ten seconds in a hurdler's stretch. She swung each leg twenty-five times, high enough to send the ball to the moon. If she was going to kick well, she needed her muscles warm. Warming up also prevented injuries.

Suddenly, Coach Brown broke the chalk in half and picked up his clipboard. As he shouted out names, players hustled toward the door. "Dupree, the wind is picking up and might be a factor. Bear that in mind. You, too, Peterson, with your passes. Keep them hard and fast. Neil, make every snap a good one."

The whole time Coach Brown barked his orders, Michelle expected some kind of reaction from Joey. After all, this was the first time this season he would not be holding or kicking. But Michelle was in for a surprise. Jocko wasn't whining to Coach.

"Did you see Jocko? He was as quiet as a sick moose,"

she commented to Matt as they trotted out of the locker room.

"Yeah, I noticed. I wonder what gives."

"Do you think he suspects?"

"That we know he sabotaged you?" Matt put his helmet on and snapped the chin strap. The white mouthpiece dangled from his face guard. "I don't know. He's acting weird, that's all I can say." He held his hand out for a high five and Michelle slapped it. "C'mon," Matt yelled, quarterback style, as he pushed the heavy school door open. "Let's focus on the game. Leave Joey for later."

Michelle jogged with the others along the gravel path behind the bleachers. When she finally saw the field, goosebumps ran up her arms. With the field lights on and the air crisp and clear, the grass glowed a bright emerald green, a beautiful contrast against the sharp white yard lines. She had to pinch herself to believe what she was seeing was real. The Eagles vs. the Barracudas wasn't a junior high game. It was the pros.

Right away the boys began warming up with team calisthenics. Michelle began kicking balls into the portable soccer net set up on the sidelines. Afterward, she practiced dropping the football in front of her as she would for a punt. The whole time she concentrated on technique and eliminating distractions. In a game situation, she couldn't listen to the crowd or even another player. To kick and punt successfully, she had to focus on herself and the ball. Not even thoughts of Sandy could get in the way.

Matt tapped her on the shoulder, and Michelle jumped a mile. "Neil's ready to snap. I'm holding. Coach wants you to hit a few field goals while both ends of the field are free."

She hit two with the wind but flubbed two against it. Coach was right. The wind was definitely a factor.

"Pregame practice doesn't mean a thing," Matt said as they walked back toward the benches. "The game is what counts. The wind caught a couple of my passes, too."

When he pointed into the stands, Michelle followed his gaze. Her mom and dad were sitting in the parents' section beside Sandy's folks. Probably Matt's parents were there, too. Brian sat several rows up with Derek and some of their high school friends. Seeing her, Derek stood up and bowed. Michelle responded by waving her helmet with one hand while giving them the victory sign with the other. That was when she spied Sandy climbing through the bleachers with her notebook and clicky pen. Quickly, Michelle signaled Brian, who scrambled after Sandy. A few minutes later, Sandy was scurrying down to where Michelle was waiting.

"I'm sorry I blew up at you," Michelle blurted.

Meanwhile, the Jefferson fans had erupted in cheers. The Eagles had begun their special pregame drill.

"It's okay." Sandy put her clicky pen in her purse. "You had a right to be upset. Being the only girl on the team is a tough position. I should have gone a lot easier on you."

"No. You're a good reporter. You called the shots as you saw them."

"Still friends?" Sandy held out her pinky.

Smiling, Michelle locked her pinky around Sandy's and pulled, a sign of lasting friendship.

"Till the end," they both said together.

"Now, go out there and smear those Barracudas," Sandy yelled.

"I will. Oh." Michelle turned. "I almost forgot to tell you. Matt and I discovered the problem with my kicking."

"You did? What?"

The crowd roared as the cheerleaders began jumping up and down. It was getting more and more difficult to hear.

Michelle cupped her hands to her mouth and shouted. "The laces were supposed to bring good luck. Jocko told me it was lucky to kick under where the laces are."

Sandy leaned forward and squinted as she strained to understand. "What? Lace? Like ruffles?" Suddenly, her eyes grew large. "Jocko wears lucky underwear? With ruffles?"

Michelle shook her head and shouted, "NO!" but she doubted Sandy heard.

Just then, the stands on both sides erupted in total frenzy. At the same time, the Jefferson cheerleaders tried to drown out the Barracuda fans with a catchy chant. Some fans threw shiny confetti as the Jefferson side stood up while the band played the school anthem.

And then the Barracudas rolled onto the field.

Michelle sucked in her breath as her stomach turned flip-flops. There ought to be a law against boys growing so big. These guys in their nasty steel helmets were positively huge! They made Jocko Joey look like a peanut. The Eagles didn't need a kicker. They needed Jack the Giant Killer.

They didn't need a game plan either. What they needed was a miracle. She and the rest of the Eagles were going to be mashed into creamed pea soup.

"Okay, guys. We can see what we're up against," Coach said when he called them over. "Don't go getting lily-livered on me."

As Michelle and the kicking team took the field, the drumroll started and built in intensity, joined by screams and cheers from the Jefferson fans. Finally, amidst a gigantic wave of noise, Michelle lofted the ball off the tee and sent it sailing down the field, where a Barracuda grabbed it and charged forward.

"Get him!" Michelle yelled. But he was already past half the team. "Get him!" she screamed again. Excited, she turned sharply and sprang into a run, ignoring the sudden twinge of pain in her ankle.

Forget what Coach had told her about running to the sidelines. Forget how that Barracuda looked like a black-and-silver tank. If she could tackle that Barracuda before he put points on the board, she would.

But there was no catching this Barracuda—not by Michelle or any other Eagle. He slid through the Eagles' grasp, twisting, dodging, and leaping over blue-and-gold uniforms until only the end zone was left.

The pandemonium on the Barracudas' side was sickening.

Stunned, Michelle and the rest of the kicking team headed back toward the benches. They expected Coach Brown would be hot, and he was. The only thing that kept him from throwing his clipboard was the video cams in the stands capturing all the action.

"Man, did you see that crummy play!" Jocko roared. "That fish put his cleats right up my back."

Finally Matt hollered, "Hey, get it together. We still have thirty-nine minutes in this game."

Michelle sat down on the bench with a thud. Holding her helmet between her knees, she bowed her head. Absentmindedly, she rotated her ankle. Every once in a while, she could feel a small twinge, then a bigger *zing*!

Crossing her legs, she reached down, grabbed her ankle, and squeezed while flexing her foot. I'll be okay, she told herself, as long as it doesn't get any worse.

CHAPTER 15

Under the intense glow of their field lights and with the west wind whipping punishment across Jefferson's field, the Eagles had given their loyal fans everything they had and more. Matt had expertly executed running and passing plays. Throwing with the wind, he had connected with Rani for two spectacular long yardage plays, sending Michelle and the fans screaming to their feet. But when he threw against the wind, the pigskin was likely to go almost anywhere, including into the Barracudas' waiting arms. Each time the Barracudas gained possession, they racked more points on the board. But sometimes when Michelle was on the field, the strong wind worked to the Eagles' advantage. Both field goal attempts, with Matt holding, were successful. Even so, at halftime they were down by seven points.

No one knew about Michelle's ankle, and even if they had, she would have said it was okay. In fact, she had even forgotten about it herself in the heat of this brutal contest against their archrivals. Keeping her muscles loose on the sidelines was her standard procedure. It wasn't until the halftime whistle blew and she began walking toward the girls' bathroom that she noticed the tenderness in her ankle. Michelle struggled not to limp. Like other coaches, Coach Brown sometimes benched his injured players. No way was she going to let that happen to her.

"Darn those Barracudas!" Michelle exploded as she collapsed in a chair Sandy had borrowed from the cafeteria and wedged into the girls' bathroom.

"How can you stand it?" Skye handed Michelle a cup of steaming hot chocolate. "Those Barracudas are like an army of programmed robots. They're awesome. They're unreal!"

"Yeah!" Michelle agreed. "No matter how deep I kick the ball, they just keep coming!"

"And clunking, and banging, and crushing," Sandy babbled. "I've got it all here." She waved her notebook. "Too bad you can't tell me what Matt says when you guys huddle. Oooh! Such a scoop!"

Michelle wasn't paying attention. Over the delicious chocolate aroma, she smelled something pleasantly familiar.

"I noticed you trying hard to hide a limp when you left the field," Miss Ashleigh said to Michelle as she walked in, surprising everyone. She set a pair of scissors and a roll of white athletic tape on the sink. Michelle allowed the teacher to gently examine her ankle. "Hurts about right here, doesn't it?"

"No, not really." Michelle winced. "Well, sort of."

"Nothing seems to be broken," Miss Ashleigh reassured her. She snapped an ice pack and indicated that Skye should hold it in place. "In a minute, I'll show you how to tape Michelle's ankle. What this girl needs is an equipment manager," she said to Skye.

"Me?" Skye sounded honored.

Miss Ashleigh winked. "We'll have to square it with Coach Charlie first, but I certainly can't see a problem with it."

Michelle choked on her cocoa while Sandy's eyes almost popped out of her head. Right away her purple clicky pen began doing double time in her little white notebook.

Scoop city!

At Miss Ashleigh's direction, Michelle propped her leg on the teacher's canvas sports bag.

"What if she has to run?" Skye watched closely as Miss Ashleigh wound the tape securely around Michelle's ankle and foot in a crisscross pattern.

"That's very unlikely." Miss Ashleigh handed the roll of tape to Skye. "That's good, Skye. Keep it nice and tight."

"But I still have to kick," Michelle said, worried. "Will I still be able to kick after I'm taped up like a mummy?"

Miss Ashleigh chuckled. "You shouldn't have any trouble, sugar. This is going to give you just the right amount of support."

"But suppose Coach sees all this tape and thinks I'm really hurt?"

"Don't you worry about that. You should have been taped prior to the game anyway, which only shows why you need an equipment manager." Miss Ashleigh slipped the tape and scissors back in her purse.

"Thanks for everything, Miss Ashleigh," Michelle said, standing up and testing her ankle. "This feels great."

The second half started with a big bang.

It was the Barracudas' turn to kick off against the wind. The Eagles receiver grabbed the ball and ran twelve yards before being pushed out of bounds by one Barracuda and tackled unnecessarily by a second. Whistles shrilled and flags flew all over the place. The Jefferson fans sent loud boos across the field.

"Unnecessary roughness!" the referee called out. "Fifteen yards! First down. Get it in play, Eagles!"

Michelle leaned forward on the bench and crossed her fingers as Matt and his offense ran onto the turf. With the wind to their backs, they were in excellent position.

"You can do it, Matt!" she yelled.

Neil snapped the ball. Matt faded back. Like a bullet, Rani shot downfield and cut sharply to the right. So did the two Barracudas who were double-covering him. Most of the other Barracudas and Eagles seemed locked in combat near the line of scrimmage. No one was going anywhere—except for Lamar, who suddenly tore a straight path near the sidelines. The Barracudas saw, but not in time. Matt threw a bullet to Lamar, who ran for twenty-five yards before being brought down.

The next two plays gave them a first down. Two more plays, another first down. Brimming with confidence, Michelle left the bench to warm up. Momentum was everything.

Michelle was kicking balls in the net, practicing for an almost certain extra point attempt, when she heard the crowd roar its disappointment.

Fumble on the seven yard line!

But instead of letting the Barracudas march back up the field for another touchdown, the Eagles blitzed and

154

sacked the Barracuda quarterback, something they'd never been able to do before.

"Jo-ey! Jo-ey! Jo-ey!" the cheerleaders chanted. The fans were so noisy the referees had to signal for quiet.

The next time Jocko sacked the quarterback, Michelle leaped to her feet—and immediately grimaced as a hint of pain shot through her ankle.

"Yea, Joey! Way to go, Jocko!" she yelled along with everyone else.

The Barracudas were forced to punt.

Three plays later, it was Michelle's turn to punt. Trotting onto the field, she hoped her foot would be okay. Just then, the Barracudas' creepy primary punt returner shoved his big head in her face.

"I dare you to kick it to me, tootsie," he jeered.

It was an old trick. He was trying to steal her concentration. "C'mon, pigtails." He beckoned with his hands. "I double dare you. Cluck, cluck, cluck. Don't be a chicken."

I'm not a chicken! I'm an Eagle! she wanted to yell, but she didn't—not because she was scared but because she was smart. Just to show the creep how smart, she walloped the ball to the secondary receiver, and an Eagle swooped down on him before he took one step.

When they switched goals at the beginning of the fourth quarter, the Eagles had drastically narrowed the gap. They could almost taste victory, but the Barracudas never let up. Except for replacing their quarterback, they didn't even look tired. Clearly, if the Eagles were going to win, Coach needed to keep his biggest, bulkiest Eagles active. Michelle watched silently as Joey began playing both offense and defense.

The clock was ticking down.

With Joey on the offensive front line, Matt had more time to find his receivers. When he handed off to Jocko, the big boy plowed roads where none existed before.

Toward the end of the fourth quarter, the score was Barracudas 19, Eagles 13, with only minutes to play. It was fourth down on the Barracudas' forty-five yard line with eight yards to go for a first down. If Matt tried to run the ball, he probably wouldn't make it. The Barracudas might expect him to throw a pass, but even with the wind on their side, Matt's pass could be intercepted—something they could not afford this late in the game.

If the Eagles wanted to win, they would have to trick the Barracudas. They would let the Barracudas think they were going to attempt a punt.

Coach signaled for the punting unit, Joey included.

Seconds later, standing almost in midfield, Michelle stared at the hulking Barracudas. Then she glanced down apprehensively at her taped ankle. She took a deep breath. As scary as it was, she knew what she had to do. This was the moment she'd dreamed about.

If Matt was on the field as quarterback or as holder, he could lead the team. But he wasn't.

She would do it.

Michelle waved the team into a huddle. After being involved in almost every play, Joey was panting. His face was a river of sweat. His torn uniform was plastered to his body. He looked like he'd been through a war. She noticed his knuckles were bruised and scraped. She'd never seen such determination in his steely blue eyes.

She wasn't their quarterback, but the Eagles needed direction, and she intended to supply it.

"Okay, guys. Listen hard. I'm going to call a fake."

"How intriguing," Rani remarked. "It will be a play we most certainly have practiced."

"Yeah," Michelle answered as she clapped her hands. "Ready. Break!"

Right away, they broke huddle and assumed their positions. She looked over her team's hunched backs toward the coveted goal line. Neil held the ball in position, ready to snap it whenever she was ready. She raised her foot slightly, giving Neil the green light.

Whap! He snapped the ball to Michelle.

"Fire!" she yelled. The Eagles dug their toes in the turf and sprang from the line of scrimmage.

"Fire! Fire! Fire!"

Everyone ran, expecting Michelle to pass—everyone except Joey, who shifted exactly in front of her with his legs spread and his elbows bent. Meanwhile, Barracudas were buzzing everywhere, looking for fresh kill. If the punter was going to pass instead of punt, they had to find the receiver and fast. In a fraction of a second, the Barracudas had most of the Eagles covered. The others were locked in a seemingly impenetrable wall of blue and gold, black and silver.

In a flash, Joey motioned with his head and rolled his huge shoulders forward. Michelle didn't need a second invitation. She followed him, tight as a shadow, while he took her through the wall to daylight.

By the time the Barracudas discovered what had happened, she had left Joey and was pumping toward the twenty. Out of the corner of her eye, she saw Coach Brown on the sidelines.

"Go, Michelle!" he hollered.

Hearing her name, she almost lost her stride.

"Dig in, girl. Fly!"

The crowd was yelling and stomping.

MI-CHELLE! *Stomp-stomp.* MI-CHELLE! *Stomp-stomp.*

Michelle put on the gas. At the same time, she glanced over her shoulder. She was being chased by a black-and-silver tornado!

Faster! Faster!

She was closing in on the five yard line.

Four, three, two, one.

She charged across the goal line.

Touchdown!

Without thinking, Michelle smacked the ball on the ground and did the funky chicken as the tornado ran out of bounds.

On the sidelines, the rest of the Eagles were jumping up and down. Blue-and-gold pom-poms sailed through the air like Roman candles on the Fourth of July. The fans were going crazy.

The score was tied, 19–19, with six seconds left on the clock. Matt was racing toward her while the kicking team set up for the extra point.

"Just like practice, Michelle!"

In a mass of confusion, Neil hiked the ball to Matt, who smoothly set it in place. Michelle began her approach. She swung her foot and connected. Right away arms flew in the air and big, wide hands tried to block her kick. But her kick was high and good, flying on Eagles' wings between the goalposts.

The final whistle sounded. 20–19, Eagles!

What a finish!

Matt's arms were around her ribcage. He was dancing and swinging her in circles. There was no time to catch her breath.

In a blur, she and the rest of the Eagles, along with Coach Brown and his assistants, rushed to congratulate the Barracudas on a game well played. Behind them, the bleachers on the Eagles' side were emptying as swarms of fans joined them on the field.

Brian was pumping her arm. "Way to go, Sis. I knew you could do it." Derek, trying hard to look cool, tapped her on the helmet.

She took her helmet off and shook out her braids. In the crush, she thought she saw Sandy, but then Matt grabbed her hand and she turned toward him instead. Brian and Derek disappeared as confetti swirled in the night sky, fell in her hair, dusted the freckles on Matt's nose.

She saw the familiar hulking shoulders and hollered with what was left of her voice. "Jocko, we have to ask you something." She pulled Matt along with her.

But before she could ask, Jocko apologized. Then he told her he'd only jinxed her partway through the Generals game. The rest of the time, she'd psyched herself out with a negative attitude. That would never happen again!

Suddenly, the ground beneath Michelle's feet shifted as a mighty roar rumbled through the crowd.

"Yea, Mi-chelle!"

Jocko and the rest of the team lifted her high on their shoulders.

Uh-oh. She'd lost her helmet. Coach would kill her for sure. Frantically, Michelle pointed and called, but the noise was too loud and no one heard. Then, out of the corner of her eye, she saw Sandy stoop down and pick it up.

But wait! Where was the team taking her?

Laughing and cheering, they carried her off the field, down the path, through the school door, and along the echoing hallway.

"Mi-chelle! Mi-chelle! Mi-chelle!"

Michelle glanced over her shoulder in time to see Sandy scurrying alongside Rani. Still, the chanting would not stop.

And then, just when she thought she'd had enough surprises for one day, there was Skye along with Miss Ashleigh standing next to Coach Brown inside the door to the boys' locker room. Coach was grinning from ear to ear and welcoming everyone in.

"Oooh-eeee! This is super!"

Michelle heard Sandy's squeal. Ponytail bouncing, her eyes wide as saucers, she checked out the locker room. She was giving Michelle the thumbs-up sign.

Laughing, Michelle raised her arms in victory.

Welcome home!

Welcome to the boys' locker room!